DO TIGERS DRINK BLOOD?

AND 13 OTHER MYSTERIES OF NATURE

Arefa Tehsin
Raza H. Tehsin

Illustrated by
Kavita Singh Kale

RED TURTLE
RUPA

Published in Red Turtle by
Rupa Publications India Pvt. Ltd 2014
7/16, Ansari Road, Daryaganj
New Delhi 110002

Sales centres:
Allahabad Bengaluru Chennai
Hyderabad Jaipur Kathmandu
Kolkata Mumbai

ISBN: 978-81-291-3123-2

First impression 2014

10 9 8 7 6 5 4 3 2 1

DO TIGERS DRINK BLOOD?

Arefa Tehsin is an author, a traveller, a columnist and the Honorary Wildlife Warden of Udaipur. Because of her naturalist father, she grew up with jungles and animals around her. She is the author of the rainforest based fantasy novel *Iora & the Quest of Five* and *The Elephant Bird*, a picture book in six languages, and co-author of *Land of the Setting Sun* and *Tales from the Wild*.

Raza H. Tehsin has spent seventy years in and out of the jungles. He has helped form three wildlife sanctuaries, reported fourteen new animals from the region and has written over a hundred research papers as well as three books on wildlife.

Kavita Singh Kale has been illustrating and writing for children's books, music videos and short films for over a decade now. She has a BFA in painting from New Delhi and a PG degree in Animation from the National Institute of Design, Ahmedabad.

Other books in the series

What if the Earth Stopped Spinning?
And 24 Other Mysteries of Science

How Did the Harappans Say Hello?
And 16 Other Mysteries of History

To the visionary T. H. Tehsin and the brave-heart
Khurshid Banu Tehsin, who taught us to seek an explanation
behind every mystery we came across in life

CONTENTS

WHY DO CROCODILES HAVE STONES IN THEIR STOMACHS?

WHAT DO YOU EXPECT YOUR STOMACH TO CONTAIN? INTESTINES, GASTRIC JUICES AND, OF COURSE, THE CAKE OR CHOCOLATE YOU JUST ATE. BUT GUESS WHAT CROCODILES HAVE IN THEIR BELLIES THAT YOU AND I DON'T—STONES!

WHY DO THEY HAVE STONES IN THEIR STOMACHS? WE'LL FIND OUT SOON. BUT FIRST LET'S GET TO KNOW THESE COOL LIZARD-LIKE, CARNIVOROUS, STURDY, HALF-AQUATIC, LARGE REPTILES BETTER.

LIZARD OF THE NILE

Crocodiles get their name from the clever ancient Greeks, who were in the habit of naming everything.

In Ancient Greek, crocodile literally means 'the lizard of the (Nile) river'. From ancient to present-day civilizations, crocodiles have been considered symbols of power. Some hunt them, others worship them. Crocodile skin is not just a fashion statement but a status symbol in tribal societies. A tribe in New Guinea revers crocodiles so much that they scar their skin to match that of the reptile. Fancy that! But don't try that at home. It's an awfully painful procedure.

Crocodile skin is traded legally and illegally across the world as it is supposed to be durable and very soft. The skin on the belly of the crocodile is used to make various commercial products like handbags and shoes. The skin on its back, on the other hand, is so hard that arrows and spears would only give the croc giggles and tickles.

WHAT BIG TEETH YOU HAVE!

CROCODILES HAVE DREADFULLY UNEVEN TEETH, SHARP AND POINTED, PERFECTLY FIT FOR CRUSHING THEIR PREY OR RIPPING A CREATURE APART. THIS COMES IN USEFUL AS A CROCODILE EATS A WIDE VARIETY OF CREATURES, FROM BIRDS, TURTLES AND FISH TO BUFFALOES, DEER, SMALLER CROCODILES, AND EVEN SHARKS AND BIG CATS. BUT ONCE IT HAS CAPTURED ITS PREY WITH THOSE POWERFUL JAWS, HOW DOES IT CHEW? THAT'S A DIFFICULT QUESTION, AS ITS TEETH ARE NOT DESIGNED FOR CHEWING. AND WHAT WOULD ONE GET IF ONE SWALLOWS SHELLS AND SKULL, HAIR AND HORNS, FEATHERS AND FLESH WITHOUT CHEWING? PERHAPS AN UPSET STOMACH TO BEGIN WITH.

EERIE EVOLUTION

Before we unravel this mystery, let's look at where crocodiles came from. They are not as rock-headed as they seem–all teeth and no brains. In fact, they're quite intelligent. What can be better evidence of their intelligence than the fact that they've survived *240 million years*, and may have even witnessed (and shed crocodile tears) on the extinction of dinosaurs! The oldest crocodile fossil is 240 million years old, from the Jurassic period, and is called Protosuchus, meaning 'first crocodile'. Crocodilians (all the species that form the order Crocodilia) belonged to the family of animals called archosaurs, or the 'ruling lizards,' from which dinosaurs and birds evolved. Between 240 to 65 million years, the ancient crocodiles lived on land, in the sea and a variety of habitats. Some earliest ones had bipedal postures and were even herbivores, eating vegetable matter. They had adapted themselves in various ways, including their eating habits, in order to survive alongside the dinosaurs.

And then, 65 million years ago, a meteor crashed into Earth and resulted in the mass extinction of the great lizards. Many types of prehistoric crocs, especially the giant ones, became extinct. The crocodiles that survived the mass extinction most likely did so by evolving different jaw shapes to adapt to feeding in various habitats and by exploiting the available food resources. Everyone can't just open the refrigerator to get food. Many have to stalk, pursue and kill, and even evolve their jaws to do so!

Today, there are fourteen species of true crocodiles found in Africa, Australia, Asia and the Americas. True crocodiles are different from alligators, caimans and gharials. These belong to separate biological families but to the same order Crocodilia, of which there are twenty-three species. All of them together are referred to as crocodilians, not crocodiles.

THIS IS HOW THEY'RE CLASSIFIED:
- Kingdom: Animalia
- Phylum: Chordata
- Class: Reptilia
- Order: Crocodilia

The order Crocodilia includes the families Crocodylidae (true crocodiles), Alligatoridae (alligators and caimans) and Gavialidae (gharials).

SENSIBLE SENSES

240 million years of evolution have earned crocodiles acute senses, which make them top-notch predators. The crocodile's eyes, ears and nostrils are located on top of the head, allowing it to be hidden from its prey while it remains almost submerged in water. Its night vision is superb and it generally hunts at night, taking advantage of the poor night vision of its prey. Its sense of smell is very well-developed. It can detect prey as well as dead animals, both in land and water, from quite some distance.

Crocodiles have sensory pits on their lower and upper jaws that look like small black spots on the skin. With the help of these detectors, known as Domed Pressure Receptors (DPRs), they detect vibration and pressure changes and can sense the slightest changes in the water—as small as a single drop! So even in total darkness the croc will know where its prey is! (This is their sense of touch.) They strike swiftly. The larger ones like the Nile crocodile and the Saltwater crocodile (the largest living reptile, this croc can reach up to 23 feet and weigh up to 1,000 kg) are dangerous to humans. Anyone with uneven teeth, and without braces or a sense of humour, would be.

BITE & FIGHT

Did you know that the Saltwater crocodile's bite is the strongest bite ever recorded? It is the largest of all reptiles on Earth and has the widest distribution of any crocodile. Australians fondly call them 'salties.' It is estimated that around two hundred humans fall prey to the jaws of the Nile crocodile each year! But these ferocious crocs are caring parents and very social as well.

A crocodile's tongue is held back by a membrane that doesn't allow it to move freely. Although crocodiles have extremely strong muscles to close the jaw, the muscles to open it are quite weak. You could just tie a rubber band to shut their jaws together. And no, not the rubber band of your ponytail, but maybe one cut from the tube of a tyre.

But don't stand there and chuckle after shutting the jaws of this big guy because a blow from its tail can knock you out cold! The powerful tail helps them to swim at speeds up to 40 km per hour. Their webbed feet help them move flexibly in water and overcome their prey by making sudden moves. They can stand underwater for hours, run rapidly for short distances and even jump several metres out of water! So forget about the guy who made up the tongue twister, 'Craig crocodile-crawled 'cross crooked crawling creepies.'

NO SWEAT

Crocodiles are cold-blooded reptiles. They absorb heat with their thick armoured skin but they don't sweat as they don't have sweat glands. Have you ever seen a croc sleeping on the land, on a mud bank or in a zoo? It sleeps with its mouth open. That's not to scare you but to release heat through its mouth.

THE MYSTERY OF THE STONES IN THE STOMACH

SO TO GET BACK TO THE 'MYSTERY' WE STARTED WITH, LET'S SEE WHAT WE HAVE LEARNT ABOUT THE CROCODILE'S EATING BEHAVIOUR. THEY HAVE A POWERFUL BITE AND THEY GULP. THEY HAVE STRONG JAWS WHICH THEY CAN OPEN WIDE AND A TONGUE THAT IS RESTRICTED IN ITS MOVEMENT. THEY ALSO HAVE A VERY SLOW METABOLISM RATE AND CAN SURVIVE WITHOUT FOOD FOR MONTHS. HOWEVER, LIKE EVERYONE ELSE, THEY NEED TO PROPERLY DIGEST THEIR MEALS. THEY DO THIS BY A TRICK THEY'VE LEARNT FROM THE DINOSAURS, (OR THE DINOSAURS HAVE LEARNT FROM THEM—WE'LL NEVER KNOW.) BUT THE TRICK IS AS OLD OR OLDER. SOME DINOSAURS IN THE GROUP SAUROPODA, CONSISTING OF THE LARGEST ANIMALS TO HAVE EVER LIVED ON OUR PLANET, APPEAR TO HAVE HAD STONES IN THEIR STOMACH TOO.

GROOVY GASTROLITHS

Crocodiles are closely related to dinosaurs. But guess what they're even more closely related to...birds! Yes, crocodiles are the closest to dinosaurs and birds than any other reptiles. They are the only reptiles that have a four-chambered heart like birds and mammals. Biologically complex is the term for them.

Warm-blooded birds need more oxygen to maintain their body temperatures and high metabolic rates. Their four-chambered hearts keep oxygenated and deoxygenated bloods separate. However, cold-blooded reptiles with low metabolic rates need less oxygen. In their three-chambered hearts, the good and bad blood get mixed up and partially oxygenated blood is supplied to the body. The remarkable crocodilian heart has an advantage in the form of a unique valve called Foramen of Panizza, which can control the blood flow towards the lungs while diving. So effectively, its four-chambered heart becomes three-chambered while diving. It makes the crocodiles lower their metabolic rate and hence need less oxygen. This way they can stay underwater for long periods of time, making them deadly predators.

They also share another biological feature with dinosaurs and some species of birds. *They swallow stones to help them digest their food*! Yes, you heard it right, stones that help them grind the food inside the stomach. These stones, that the crocodiles swallow are known as gastroliths or stomach stones, as they're held inside the stomach.

The word 'gastrolith' derives from the Greek words *gastro* meaning stomach and *lithos* meaning stone. Crocodiles aren't the only ones who have them. Gastroliths are also found in other animals like seals, sea lions and certain birds. Some dinosaurs had them too. These stones rest in the muscular gizzard of animals that lack proper grinding teeth and are used to grind the food.

Crocodiles also use these stomach stones or gastroliths as ballast, or extra weight, to balance their bodies while swimming and to decrease buoyancy.

The size of these stomach stones depends on the body weight of the animal. Some gastroliths associated with dinosaur fossils can weigh several kilograms. The stones swallowed by ostriches can be longer than 10 cm. These stones can either be rounded and polished or with rough edges.

The stomach of a crocodile is divided into two chambers. One is muscular, like a bird's gizzard, and the other is acidic. It is the most acidic digestive system of any vertebrate in the world! This stomach can digest almost anything from nails to hooves, bones to feathers. The gastroliths are found in the first muscular stomach. These stones, swallowed by crocodiles at leisure, crush the bones, hooves and other such tough matter in the first stomach. The bones may lie in the first stomach for days till they're properly crushed and sent to the next chamber, where they're digested with the strong acidic juices. Talk about not wasting your food!

On an average, a crocodile lives between thirty to eighty years, depending on the species. There is one crocodile in an Australian zoo that is estimated to be 130 years old! Crocodiles carry the gastroliths throughout their lives.

CROCODILE TEARS

If you thought having stones in its stomach is the crocodile's coolest feature, think again! Have you heard of the term 'crocodile tears'? The old myth says that crocodiles weep while eating humans. Now while it is true that crocodiles do tear up, that is just a physical function of their body. Their eyes froth and bubble while eating. Maybe it would be better to call them tears of joy!

LEAVE ME ALONE

With their fearsome hunting abilities, tough physical features and the fact that they have outlived dinosaurs, shouldn't crocodiles be invincible? Sadly, this is not true. Although crocodiles have survived multiple mass extinctions, including those of dinosaurs, many species today are listed as critically endangered and on the verge of extinction.

We humans are responsible for their state. We're destroying their river and wetland homes, building our cities over these. Many of us pay huge amounts of money to buy illegal crocodile-skin products like purses, belts, wallets and shoes.

Besides this, another reason for some types of crocodiles being endangered is that the survival rate of crocodile hatchlings is very low. Crocodiles lay eggs in nests (are you thinking birds again?) made of dug out sand or vegetation. Depending on the species, the nesting period may be a few weeks to six months. The mother comes to know the eggs are about to hatch when the little ones start calling out from inside the eggs! Sometimes the croc mum takes the eggs out of the nest and rolls them on the ground to help the little ones come out. Other than their egg-cries before they're born, the hatchlings also have an 'egg-tooth', made out of skin at the tip of their snouts which help them break the shell when they're ready.

Once they're out, the croc mum carries them in her mouth to the water. (A group of hatchlings is called a crèche or a pod.) But ninety-nine per cent of hatchlings die in their first year. That is the time they're most vulnerable and end up being eaten as snacks by monitor lizards, other crocodiles, large fish and even birds like herons.

Crocodiles keep the rivers clean by eating carcasses and balancing the population of other species. They're both predator and prey, as their little ones get eaten by other hunters of the wild. Nutrients are recycled between land and aquatic ecosystems through these reptiles, which keeps ecosystems healthy.

It's a matter of great sadness that these awesome reptiles are becoming fewer and fewer in number, thanks to us. Steve Irvin, also called the Crocodile Hunter, had once said, 'Take the crocodiles...my favourite animal. There are twenty-three species. Seventeen of those species are rare or endangered. They're on their way out, no matter what anyone does or says, you know.'

Crocodiles, who survived the dinosaurs, might not be able to survive humankind! They are, today, our cold-blooded victims.

COOL CROC FACTS

* EVEN WHEN A CROC IS ALMOST SUBMERGED IN WATER TO HIDE FROM ITS PREY, ITS EYES, EARS AND NOSE, WHICH ARE PLACED HIGH UP ON THE SKULL, REMAIN OUT OF WATER. WHAT A SLY HUNTER!

* A PROTECTIVE MEMBRANE CLOSES OVER THE EYES OF THE CROC WHEN IT'S SUBMERGED IN WATER. JUST LIKE YOUR SWIMMING GOGGLES.

* CROCODILES ARE THE MOST SOCIAL REPTILES OF ALL.

* THE PREHISTORIC CROC SARCOSUCHUS, ALSO CALLED SUPER-CROC, WAS 40 FEET LONG AND ATE DINOSAURS.

* THE SLIGHTLY SMALLER PREHISTORIC CROC DEINOSUCHUS DERIVES ITS NAME FROM THE SAME ROOT AS THE DINOSAURS (WELL, YES, GREEK): *DINO* MEANING 'TERRIBLE'.

WHY IS A BUTCHER BIRD NAMED SO?

THERE IS A BUTCHER AMONG BIRDS TOO. WHAT DOES IT DO TO
HAVE GAINED THIS NICKNAME? BIRDS ARE PERHAPS THE MOST
FASCINATING OF ALL FAUNA TO BE FOUND ON EARTH. TAKE A LOOK
AT THESE CHARACTERISTICS OF SOME BIRDS:
THE MAGPIE IS A SINGER, THE KINGFISHER A DIVER, THE ROOSTER
AN EARLY RISER, THE VULTURE A SCAVENGER, THE PEACOCK A
DANCER, THE SPARROW A HOPPER, THE CROW A TOOL USER,
THE EAGLE A GLIDER AND THE OWL A SILENT FLIER.

BUT WHAT IS THE SHRIKE?
DO STABBINGS AND HANGING THE DEAD GIVE YOU A CLUE?

WHO IS THE BUTCHER BIRD?

The shrike is a butcher bird. Butcher birds, or different species
of shrikes, are largely insect-eaters but the larger ones also prey
on lizards, mice and other small vertebrates. They have a creepy
habit of impaling their prey on the thorns or crevices of trees! If
you look closely inside a bush or a tree frequented by a shrike,
you might see bodies of insects, lizards, small birds or mice—
depending on the size and species of shrike—hanging there with
a thorn jutting out in the middle. The shrike is a territorial bird
and guards its area fiercely. It generally hunts in its own territory.

It sits upright on an exposed perch to search for the prey and warn other shrikes to watch out before entering its domain. Once it spots and catches an unsuspecting prey, it hammers its head with its hooked, strong beak to kill it. It also pierces the prey to attract mates! Sound sufficiently gruesome for you?

WHY ON EARTH?

THE BUTCHER BIRD DOESN'T DO THIS FOR FUN, EVEN THOUGH THE BIRD MAY LOOK LIKE A MASKED BANDIT WITH THE BLACK STRIPE RUNNING ACROSS ITS FOREHEAD AND EYES. IT IMPALES THE PREY EITHER FOR SUPPORT WHILE IT EATS IT OR FOR LATER CONSUMPTION IF IT IS FULL. THESE BIRDS ARE NO BIRD-BRAINS. IN FACT, INTELLIGENCE IN BIRDS IS WELL-DOCUMENTED. THE CROW, CONSIDERED ONE OF THE MOST INTELLIGENT CREATURES ON EARTH, CAN NOT ONLY USE BUT EVEN MAKE TOOLS TO OBTAIN FOOD! SIMILARLY THE EGYPTIAN VULTURE IS KNOWN TO BREAK EGGS OF LARGE BIRDS WHICH THEY CAN'T CARRY. THEY USE PEBBLES TO BREAK THESE EGGS AND EAT THE JUICY INSIDES.

BIRD ROMANCE

Many male birds use interesting methods to attract the females during mating season. In some birds like the weaver baya, the male constructs an elaborately woven nest to attract a female. The female answering his call comes to inspect the nest before she accepts the proposal. A peacock dazzlingly displays his tail while the female observes and approves or disapproves of him. The shrike male also has to prove his worth. He collects a cache of different objects and shows it off to the female. The collection may not only contain bodies of insects and other small creatures, but also brightly coloured decorative items. The male also chirps a musical note, quite different from its shrill cry during the mating season. It may even feed the female or perform a dance for her!

IF A MALE IS ABLE TO PERSUADE A FEMALE AFTER ALL HIS HARD WORK AND ANTICS, THEY BUILD A NEST. THE SHRIKE NEST IS CUP-SHAPED, MADE WITH LEAVES, GRASS, WOOL, FEATHERS, RAGS, HAIRS, PAPER, TWIGS, ROOTS, SHOOTS—YOU GET THE DRIFT—ANYTHING THEY CAN LAY THEIR HOOKED BEAKS ON AND HELD TOGETHER BY A COBWEB. THE NESTS OF VARIOUS SHRIKE SPECIES ARE MADE SIMILARLY. ONCE THE YOUNG ONES HATCH, THEY HEARTILY FEED ON INSECTS, LIZARDS AND OTHER YUMMIES BROUGHT IN (AND SOMETIMES CHEWED FIRST TO MAKE TENDER) BY MAMMA AND PAPA SHRIKE.

DON'T MAKE FACES. YOU HAVE NO IDEA WHAT YOUR MAMMA AND PAPA FED YOU WHEN YOU WERE A BABY!

INSECTS AND BIRDS

Now before you shake your head and say, 'These butcher birds are such butchers!', let's examine what a great favour these insect-eating birds do us.

Do you know who the most prolific breeders in nature are? No, we're not talking about humans. It's insects! New species of insects are discovered every day, as if the existing 30,000 plus species present in India alone were not enough already!

How does this matter to us? When you spot a cockroach

in the kitchen what do you do? Other than run screaming to a parent? You have regular pest control in your homes to keep unwanted insect populations in check. (Don't be too sure, though. For every cockroach you see in your kitchen, they say there are a hundred that you can't!) So what is the mechanism by which the multitude of insects, whose numbers will otherwise keep growing, kept under control in nature? The high-tech, state-of-the-art, maintenance free, insect-eating device that has been provided by nature is–birds!

Still don't believe me? Okay, let's conduct some experiments:

EXPERIMENT NO. 1

Breed a pair of drosophila (a genus of small flies) in ideal conditions. Ideal conditions mean that all the eggs are hatched, half of them are male and half female, and all survive. Don't do this in your room. The conditions won't be ideal then–either for you (because of your mum) or for the drosophila. In a single season the fly can go through twenty-five generations. A single pair can result in so many drosophila that if you compress them in a ball with 1,000 drosophila per centimetre, the diameter of this ball will be from the earth to the sun!

EXPERIMENT NO. 2

Let's take a pair of chinch bugs (pest bugs found in North America) this time and breed them in ideal conditions for one season. They can breed thirteen generations in a single season. By the time they reach the twelfth generation, we can line them up in a straight line, with ten chinch bugs per inch, in a line so long that if you travel from one end at the speed of light (1,85,000 miles per second) it'll take you *2,500 years* to reach the other end. Now don't ask how many generations you will develop in this travel time!

EXPERIMENT NO. 3

Breed a pair of cabbage aphid (a destructive insect also known as 'plant lice' in Britain) for one season. By the end of the season you would be reading this book sitting in Mars or some other planet, as the weight of these aphids would be three times the weight of all humans in the world put together! There would be no place left for humans to live on earth.

All this sound too improbable? Or do you think 'ideal conditions' is a vague term? Can it really happen the way it has been shown above?

Then here is another example just to convince you: On a 3,300-acre farm in South Africa, locusts were allowed to lay eggs without any outside interference. These eggs were dug out and they weighed 14 tonnes! 1,250 million locusts would have hatched out of those eggs if they were not removed.

THE POWER OF INSECTS

Insects have much more power than to just give you a scare. Many of them do enormous damage to vegetation. A few examples:

- Silk worms may not be that silky, but they're silky-smooth eaters. In fifty-six days, a single silk worm eats 86,000 times its weight at the time of hatching!
- Some flesh-eating larvae can eat 200 times their own weight in just one day!
- A pair of chinch bugs (about whom we spoke in experiment number two) is more powerful than the thermo-nuclear bombs of all countries put together! The human race may survive the nuclear bomb, but if chinch bugs reproduce in ideal conditions, there'll be no place left for humans to inhabit the earth!

THE POWER OF BIRDS

What are birds? Birds are vertebrate, warm-blooded, feathered bipeds. Birds are also nature's finest custom-designed way to check the growth of insects.

Their primary mode of locomotion is flight. You need more energy to run than to walk. Aeroplanes require more fuel to fly than cars require to run. Similarly, birds require a lot of energy to fly. They get this from insects (their very own protein bars) most of the times.

Most birds are insectivores. They not only eat insects but the larvae and eggs as well.

One mamma and papa starling pair bring food like caterpillars and grasshoppers to their nestlings 370 times a day. Imagine if your mamma was nagging you to eat not three times, but 370 times daily!

One mamma and papa house sparrow bring food to their nestling 260 times a day.

One mamma, papa and their chick tits, as observed and estimated by an ornithologist in Germany, destroy 120 million insect eggs per year!

OTHER BIRD SUPERPOWERS

Like bees, birds pollinate flowers and also disperse seeds. Dodos–before it was 'dead as a dodo', or extinct–used to eat the fruits of a native tree found on the island where it lived. The fruit had a very hard shell, but the dodo's strong gizzard could dissolve it. The seeds passed with its poop, got dispersed and sprouted. This was how the plant thrived in its habitat. However, once the dodo was dead due to hunting by humans, this tree also vanished from the island as its seeds were no longer dispersed.

An owl hunts two to three mice per night. Does it hunt mice because it's wise? Or is it wise because it hunts mice? In any case, mice are among the most widespread vermin that live among humans.

Vultures clean the environment by eating dead animals . If the corpses are left to rot in cities, villages and jungles, it would not only spread a foul smell but also many diseases.

All those superheroes you love reading about or watching, who know how to fly, have learnt it from the birds. Who else knows how to fly? But seriously, the earliest inventors of airplanes took many a leaf–or feather–from the birds' book of flying. They observed flight patterns and methods of taking off and landing and tried to replicate these in the aircraft they were creating. After World War II, when air travel became more widespread, engineers created wide-bodied airplanes. But how could they land these heavy planes on short runways? They thought of heavy-bodied vultures. Vultures land their large bodies on a small space and take off in a few steps! Since they couldn't study the difficult to spot superheroes (always pretending to be average in the day time), they studied the landing and take-off patterns of vultures instead. By studying how the vultures tilt their primaries–the long flight feathers along the outer edge of the wing connected to the bird's 'hand'–they built heavy-bodied planes successfully. The primaries provide thrust in a bird's flight. They can be individually rotated as well to control direction, air resistance and lift. The wings of the aircraft were crafted in a similar manner to control and provide a stable flight.

GOING...GOING...NOT YET GONE

Sadly, bird numbers are declining rapidly worldwide. Ninety-seven per cent of vultures vanished from India in just a decade! Their decline started in the 1990s due to the use of a drug called diclofenac given to livestock. It proved to be fatal for the vultures that ate these diclofenac containing dead animals. Other birds are dying due to the destruction of their living quarters, i.e. the cutting of trees where they build their nests. There is a lot of commercial fishing in lakes and ponds and fish-eating birds like cormorants and pelicans, which solely rely on fish, are dying. Insecticides used by farmers are killing the insects in the fields and not enough is left for the birds to eat. In fact, a lot of birds die of poisoning from eating insects that have been killed using insecticides. Fruits and berries are harvested widely for human consumption leaving very little for fruit-eating birds.

They say birds would be happy without humans on earth. But we wouldn't be much happier without birds. Who's going to sing songs in the morning or dance when it rains and eat all those creepy crawlies and the dead rotten mice? Not us for sure!

SO WHY DON'T YOU STEP OUTSIDE WITH YOUR TEACHER OR MAMMA OR PAPA AND TRY TO IDENTIFY AT LEAST FIVE DIFFERENT BIRDS? WHO KNOWS, YOU MIGHT BE ABLE TO SPOT A BUTCHER BIRD TOO. IF YOU'RE LUCKY, IT MAY EVEN TREAT YOU WITH ITS MIMICRY. OH YES, THE BUTCHER IS A GREAT MIMIC AS WELL! SINCE IT BARELY KNOWS YOU, IT MAY NOT MIMIC YOU. BUT IF YOU GIVE IT A PATIENT EAR, ESPECIALLY DURING ITS MATING SEASON, YOU MAY HEAR IT MIMIC THE PARROT OR THE ROOSTER OR EVEN A DRAMATIC CRY OF PAIN OF A SQUIRREL BEING CARRIED AWAY BY A HAWK—ALL TO IMPRESS THE FEMALE! THIS BIRD IS

CERTAINLY A MOST COLOURFUL CHARACTER—NOT ONLY DOES IT HAVE AN INTERESTING MANNER OF HUNTING AND CONSUMING ITS PREY, IT ALSO CONFUSES EVERYONE AROUND BY SOUNDING LIKE MANY OTHER CREATURES! WOULDN'T IT BE A SHAME IF THE SHRIKES WERE TO VANISH ONE DAY?

BOLD BIRD FACTS

* WHICH IS THE MOST COMMON BIRD ON THE PLANET? CHICKEN!
* HUMMINGBIRDS CAN FLY BACKWARDS AND BEAT THEIR WINGS AS FAST AS 80 TIMES PER SECOND!
* A TURKEY VULTURE DEFENDS ITSELF BY VOMITING ITS FOUL-SMELLING, SEMI-DIGESTED MEAL!
* THE SMALLEST BIRD IN THE WORLD IS THE BEE HUMMINGBIRD OF CUBA!
* THE ELEPHANT BIRD, WHICH BECAME EXTINCT IN THE SEVENTEENTH CENTURY, WAS AT THAT TIME THE LARGEST BIRD IN THE WORLD, REACHING MORE THAN 10 FEET IN HEIGHT!

WHY DOES THE HARE EAT ITS OWN DROPPINGS?

YES, YOU READ THAT RIGHT, THE HARE EATS ITS OWN DROPPINGS. THERE IS NO MYSTERY ABOUT IT. THE MYSTERY IS *WHY* WOULD ANYONE DO THAT? ONE WOULD THINK IT IS INCREDIBLY UNHEALTHY, NOT TO MENTION DISGUSTING. WHAT CAN POSSIBLY MAKE SOMEONE EAT ITS OWN FAECES? SURELY ONE WOULD NOT DO THAT FOR TASTE, OR FOR FUN, OR TO SHOW OFF TO FRIENDS, OR TO TEASE ONE'S MUM. THEN *WHY?*

MAYBE YOU ARE WIGGLING YOUR NOSE, PULLING A FACE AND SAYING, 'RABBITS ARE GROSS!' WELL, LET'S FIND OUT WHAT THE EXPLANATION IS FOR THIS MYSTERY. HOWEVER, BEFORE WE DO THAT, LET'S FIRST FIND OUT WHAT KIND OF CREATURES HARES ARE AND HOW THEY ARE DIFFERENT FROM RABBITS, THOUGH BOTH THESE ANIMALS EAT THEIR OWN POOP!

HARE OR RABBIT?

If Alice was from India, she would've followed a hare not a rabbit down the tree hole. True rabbits are not found in India. We only have hares here. *Khargosh* in Hindi, *sasa* in Marathi, *mola* in Kannada, *musal* in Tamil, *choura pilli* in Telugu, *moilu* in Malayalam–these are all local names of hares, not rabbits.

Both hare and rabbit belong to the Leporidae family and are herbivorous. Yet, there are a number of differences between them.

- HARES ARE LARGER IN SIZE THAN RABBITS.
- RABBITS CAN BE KEPT AS PETS BUT NOT HARES. HARES HAVEN'T BEEN DOMESTICATED.
- THE HIND LEGS OF HARES ARE LONGER THAN THOSE OF RABBITS. THAT MAKES HARES MORE RAPID RUNNERS THAN RABBITS. THE EUROPEAN BROWN HARE CAN REACH A SPEED OF 35 MILES PER HOUR! WHEN THEY SENSE DANGER, THEY CAN RUN IN A ZIGZAG MANNER TO FOOL THE ENEMY. THEY CAN JUMP VERY HIGH TOO...UP TO SEVERAL FEET!
- RABBITS ARE ADAPTED TO DIGGING AND GIVE BIRTH TO THEIR YOUNG IN BURROWS. HARES GIVE BIRTH IN RELATIVELY OPEN AREAS, IN SHALLOW DEPRESSIONS OR GRASS NESTS CALLED 'FORMS'.
- RABBITS ARE BORN BLIND AND ALMOST NAKED, WHILE HARES ARE BORN FURRY WITH OPEN EYES. THE FUR AND OPEN EYES IN YOUNG HARES MAKE UP FOR THE LACK OF PHYSICAL PROTECTION IN THEIR GRASS NESTS. THEY CAN FEND FOR THEMSELVES SOON AFTER BIRTH UNLIKE THE YOUNG RABBITS, WHICH NEED BURROWS AND MORE PROTECTION.
- UNLIKE RABBITS, WHO ARE SOCIAL ANIMALS, HARES USUALLY LIVE BY THEMSELVES AND DON'T PREFER COMPANY.

RATS! DON'T SAY THAT!

Rabbits and hares resemble rodents and were thought to be their relatives till the early twentieth century. Squirrels, mice, rabbits—all furry little things with two jutting teeth—get the resemblance? Then scientists realized that they have to think harder and look deeper beyond the obvious resemblances that even a ten-year-old can see. When they looked deeper, inside the mouth of hares and rabbits to be exact, they found that there were four incisors (cutting teeth) instead of two in the upper jaw—a large pair in front and a smaller one at the back! Also, hares and rabbits are strictly herbivores, unlike rodents, many of which eat meat as well. This led them to decide that mice and squirrels were not related to rabbits and hares and they were classified as a different order.

However, there is one similarity between rodents like mice, beavers and squirrels and leporids like hares and rabbits–their front teeth grow lifelong! These strong incisors, used to chew and cut vegetable matter, need to be kept in check from growing out of control. So they cut and chew vegetable matter with it to keep them in check. Simple! Rabbits and hares can chew in a side-to-side motion which also helps to check the growth of the back teeth. Remember how the Easter bunny is always eating a carrot? What did you think that was for?

WHY DO THEY EAT POOP?

Hares and rabbits produce two kinds of droppings. One is the faecal pellets, hard and oval in shape–the ones that you generally see if you have a pet rabbit. It doesn't eat them. The other one is called Cecotropes or 'night faeces'. These are black in colour, and runny and smelly too! These are the ones that they eat! Hares are nocturnal. They're most active from dusk to dawn. Since the 'night faeces' are passed at night, hares and rabbits eat it during the night.

RABBITS AND HARES CAN'T NIBBLE ON GRASS AND OTHER VEGETATION AT LEISURE IN THE OPEN AREAS AS THEY HAVE MANY PREDATORS LIKE HAWKS, FOXES, JACKALS, DOGS, EAGLES, WILD CATS AND HUMANS! THEY ARE IMPORTANT FOOD FOR MANY ANIMALS. SO THEY NEED TO EAT THEIR FOOD IN A HURRY! THEY QUICKLY EAT THE HERBS, SHOOTS, FRUITS, LEAVES, ROOTS, ETC. AND RUN FOR COVER. THESE PLANT MATTERS ARE HARD TO DIGEST. TO REMAIN HEALTHY AND DIGEST ALL THE NUTRIENTS PROPERLY, HARES RECYCLE THEIR FOOD A SECOND TIME BY EATING THEIR OWN POOP. THE CECOTROPES

OR 'NIGHT FAECES' ARE LOADED WITH NUTRIENTS AND WHO KNOWS, MIGHT BE TASTY TOO!

DON'T TRY THIS WITH YOUR ICE CREAM AND CHOCOLATES THOUGH— EATING THEM QUICKLY AT NIGHT AND THEN WAITING TO INGEST THEM AGAIN IN THE MORNING! YOU MIGHT NOT FIND THEM AS TASTY.

HIPPITY HOPPITY HARE

Hares and rabbits do have some features that help them outwit their hunters. They have long hind legs which they use to hop away. Their long ears detect distant sounds of an approaching predator. Their eyes, that are placed on either side of their head, give them a 360 degree vision. The ears of hares found in tropical and hot climates are longer than those that live in areas with a colder climate. This is not because the ones in the hotter climates are hard of hearing, but because larger ears help them to disperse excess body heat. The bigger the ear, the cooler the hare.

Hares can lie very still in the daytime and you can't really detect a hare unless you stumble upon it. Then it darts away very fast. It may stop after hopping for a while to look at you. Also, the large eyes take in enough light so that they can see properly in the dark hours when they are active.

MAD AS A MARCH HARE

Male hares are called bucks.
Female hares are called does.
Baby hares are called leverets.
A group of hares is called a drove.
And March hares are called mad!

So what happens to the solitary, shy hare in March? Around March, which is spring time and their mating season, hares are seen chasing each other in the meadows and having boxing matches, striking each other with their paws!

This appears to be a competition between the male hares for dominance. The one that chases the other away will be left to impress the females of the area.

ARE HARES AND RABBITS CHINESE?

Bits of jaw bones and teeth have been found in China of a kind of ground-dwelling herbivore. So scientists have been scratching their heads and wondering if the hares' mother's mother's mother originated in China. She may have. Fossils and other evidence point to the ancestors of rabbits and hares originating in Asia, possibly in the China region.

In fact, the hare is a part of traditional beliefs and folklore in China and many other parts of the world. There is no clear reason why the hare appears in folklore. It can be due to its wide distribution and numbers, or its curious features and eating habits.

Have you seen the dark spots on the moon, particularly one that resembles an old woman? Well, the Chinese believe that the old woman who sits hunched in the moon is actually a hare!

Even the Japanese and the Mexican believe that the dark patches on the moon is the outline of a hare. In African folk tales, the hare is often the trickster. In Ireland, a hare is associated with a fairy. The constellation Lepus is in the shape of a hare.

In England, there is a legend of a White Hare. It is said that a white hare narrates a story of another white hare who takes the form of a witch at night. This witch goes looking for some unsuspecting loony who finds white hares cute. Or the witch, who is actually the white hare, goes looking for the spirit of a maiden who haunts her unfaithful lover. We are not sure what the witch will do once she finds what she's looking for. We don't even know if this white hare who's telling the story is actually that witch or just a story-telling white hare!

HARE-BRAINED HARE HUNTERS

Not long ago, people in India employed a few wacky ways to hunt the poor hare. Some consider it to be a pest and think that the population needs to be kept in control in order to save standing crops. Of course, the hare is also hunted for its meat. And for its blood.

Some believe that the Indian hare's blood is supposed to cure typhoid. So when a hare is killed, they soak cotton with its blood and leave it to dry. When someone gets typhoid, they put the dry cotton in water to get the blood and treat the patient. Sounds pretty awful, right?

Since the hare is so clever at hiding from its predators, humans have come up with all kinds of pretty nasty ways to capture it. Here are a few:

- Snares.
- On a full moon night, people hide in the shadow of a large tree in a pasture. When the hares come out to eat the grass one or two may come grazing towards the shadow. The humans then throw a stone somewhere close to the hare to make it come into the shadow from the moonlight to avoid a possible predator. Then they kill the unsuspecting creature by hitting it with a lathi.
- Two people walk in the wilderness at night with an erect bamboo mat. A lantern hangs at the front of the mat and the men walk behind the mat in the shadow, so that they can't be seen. One walks holding the mat and the other holds a lathi in one hand and ghunghroos in another. Hares get attracted to this strange sound and the light aura and approach the mat out of curiosity. As soon as one is near, the man whacks it with his lathi.

Hares are hunted in other parts of world too, for their meat, which is quite lean with very little fat content. Jugged hare is a classic hare recipe made in England and France.

HOW TO MAKE JUGGED HARE

STEP 1: CATCH YOUR OWN HARE!

STEP 2: REMOVE ITS INTESTINE AND OTHER ENTRAILS.

STEP 3: HANG IT IN THE LARDER UPSIDE DOWN.

STEP 4: DRAIN THE BLOOD FROM ITS CHEST.

STEP 5: CUT IT INTO PIECES.

STEP 6: COOK THE MARINATED HARE WITH RED WINE AND JUNIPER BERRIES IN A LONG EARTHEN JUG AND LET IT STAND IN A PAN OF WATER FOR SEVERAL HOURS.

STEP 7: ADD THE HARE'S BLOOD (DON'T TELL ME YOU'VE THROWN IT AWAY!) AND SERVE THE COOKED HARE WITH PORT WINE.

STEP 8: EAT THE JUGGED HARE.

The hare is an extremely important part of the food chain and the ecosystem. It is found widely, breeds a lot and is plentiful in many parts of the world. Numerous carnivores, big and small, hunt the hare. Sometimes the bigger carnivores secure a hare to eat if they can't lay their paws on a bigger meal.

Humans, who relish eating hare, have always had a fascination for this little creature hopping around in the wild, maybe because of its ability to reproduce quickly or simply because of its cute looks. Perhaps that's the reason hares have always been presented as gifts of love. You can present a hare to your teacher. But if you want to gift your teacher a rattle snake instead, don't take this suggestion seriously.

PERPLEXING POOP FACTS

* COPROPHAGIA IS THE TERM USED FOR CONSUMPTION OF FAECES. GUESS WHERE IT'S DERIVED FROM? GREEK! IT CAN REFER TO EATING YOUR OWN POOP, OR OF OTHERS OF YOUR

KIND OR OF TOTALLY DIFFERENT ANIMALS.

* SOME INSECTS, INCLUDING A FEW BUTTERFLIES, EAT POOP OF LARGER ANIMALS. DUNG BEETLE, AS THE NAME SUGGESTS, IS A POOP-EATING INSECT. THE MOST COMMON ONE IS THE FLY!

* CATTLE IN THE US ARE FED CHICKEN LITTER AS A SOURCE OF PROTEIN.

* THE YOUNG OF ANIMALS LIKE ELEPHANTS, PANDAS AND HIPPOS EAT THEIR MOTHER'S FAECES TO OBTAIN BACTERIA TO DIGEST THEIR FOOD. GORILLAS EAT THEIR OWN AND OTHER GORILLAS' FAECES FOR BETTER ABSORPTION OF NUTRIENTS.

* PIGS, OF COURSE, EAT FAECES OF OTHER ANIMALS, AS WELL AS THEIR OWN. 'PIG TOILETS', AN AGE-OLD METHOD OF FEEDING PIGS ON HUMAN POOP AND GARBAGE, WAS USED IN CHINA.

IS THE RHINO'S HORN FAKE?

YOU CAN GET FAKE BARBIE DOLLS, FAKE HAIR COLOUR, FAKE
NAILS, FAKE FLOWERS, FAKE STOMACH ACHE (IF YOU WANT TO SKIP
SCHOOL), SPORT A FAKE SMILE, EVEN SHED A FAKE TEAR. BUT HOW
DO YOU GROW A FAKE HORN? THAT'S A REALLY DIFFICULT THING TO
DO, UNLESS YOU'RE AN ALIEN OR A MAGICIAN OR A MAGICAL ALIEN
OR AN ALIEN MAGICIAN. YET, RHINOCEROSES HAVE DONE IT. BUT
WHAT DO WE MEAN BY A FAKE HORN? THERE'S ONLY ONE WAY TO
FIND OUT: READ ON.

WHO IS THE RHINO, REALLY?

The rhinoceros is neither a magician nor an alien. It is an
ungulate or a hoofed animal. There are two types of ungulates—
even-toed ungulates (Artiodactyla) and odd-toed ungulates
(Perissodactyla). Even-toed ungulates are cattle, deer, goat, pig
and many others. Odd-toed ungulates include horse, tapir and
rhinoceros.

In the Tertiary Period (from 65 million to 1.806 million years
ago) there were more odd-toed ungulates, like jungle-dwelling
Palaeotheres and massively built Brontotherus. Most of these
herbivores became extinct with the increasing height and
coarseness of grasses, which their simple stomachs, couldn't
digest. The even-toed ungulates, with their complex stomachs
better adapted to change and became prominent. This group

has a unique arrangement of toes. If you draw a line through the middle, it will pass through the third and fourth toe. The two middle toes are large and equal in size. It looks as if a single hoof has been split in two. The rhinoceros has three toes, the horse has one functional toe and the tapir has four. Four? Isn't that even or is my calculation odd? Yes, the tapir has an even number of toes, but is an odd-toed ungulate as it has three toes on the hind feet and four on the front feet

Odd-toed ungulates are Old World animals, except the tapir, which is found in South and Central America. Old World doesn't literally mean an old world. It means Asia, Africa and Europe—the world as it was known before the 'discovery' of the Americas, which is the New World.

A FEW RHINO FACTS

The rhino is large in size with solid bones, thick skin and stumpy legs. They have existed on earth for more than 50 million years.

There are only five kinds of rhinos found in Asia and Africa but they are very different from each other. Even the Black and White rhinos of Africa separated from each other and became distinct species a million years ago!

All the rhino species weigh at least a ton (white rhinos can weigh over 3.5 tonnes!) and are one of the last remaining *megafauna* or the giant animals that existed on earth.

They are herbivores and eat grasses and leaves. Their habitats differ from each other depending on their habitats. For example, while the Indian One Horned Rhino prefers grasslands and swamps, due to its partiality towards eating grass with its well-suited grinding teeth, the Javan Rhino prefers browsing more than grazing due to its low-crowned grinding teeth. Therefore it inhabits tree forests more than grasslands.

Rhinos are large, but they're not slow. A charging rhinoceros can reach a speed of 35 miles per hour, more than double the speed achieved by the world's fastest human. And what's more, they run on their toes!

In relation to their big bodies, they have small brains (only 400-600 gm of brain weight compared to the 1,000+ kg of body weight).

Rhinos have a life span of thirty-five to forty years and the gestation period (pregnancy) lasts around sixteen months.

Although rhinos, especially male rhinoceroses, generally stay alone, they are sometimes seen in groups as well. A group of rhinos is called a crash.

BLACK, WHITE...OR GREY?

Any guesses about who named rhinoceroses? Yes, those old busybodies—the Greek. *Rhino* means nose and *ceros* means horn.

The rhinoceros's horn is such a distinctive feature that many other creatures with funny appendages on their nose also got named rhinoceros! For example, there's the rhinoceros cockroach, the rhinoceros viper, the rhinoceros iguana, the rhinoceros rat snake, the rhinoceros beetle, the rhinoceros hornbill...well, you get the drift.

There are five kinds of rhinos found in different regions of the world:

THE WHITE RHINO
Where: Africa
Horns: Two
The White rhino is not really white! They were called 'weit' meaning *wide-mouthed* in Afrikaans. If that sounds a bit rude, it is because they have flat wide lips for easy grazing. There is no conclusive explanation for the name 'white rhino' but 'weit' might have been mistaken for 'white' and although it is grey, the name White stuck. It's the largest of all rhinos. The largest recorded size of a White rhino is 4,500 kg! Perhaps 'The Hulk' would have been a better name!

THE BLACK RHINO
Where: Africa
Horns: Two
The Black rhino is not black in colour either! Then why is it called so? No one knows for sure. It is smaller than the White rhino and has special long, pointed, prehensile lips. It can even feed on leaves of thorny bushes and pick a small leaf from a twig.

THE SUMATRAN RHINO
Where: Asia
Horns: Two
This is the oldest living rhino in the world. Its relatives were the extinct woolly rhinos that roamed the earth 15 million years ago. It's the most hairy of all the rhinoceroses. What are you grinning at? Don't forget the hairy apes you've evolved from!

THE JAVAN RHINO
Where: Asia
Horns: One
One of the most endangered large mammals of the world,

it was once also found in India. But now, only sixty or fewer are left in Vietnam and Java (Indonesia).

THE INDIAN RHINO (GREATER ONE-HORNED RHINO)
Where: Asia

Horns: One

One of the largest rhinos, the India rhino is the fifth largest land animal. It has heavy folds of skin before and behind the shoulders and in front of the thighs. This gives it a cool shielded, armoured look. Its flanks and shoulders are studded with round warts. Once found from Pakistan to Burma, now most of the Indian rhinos are confined to Kaziranga National Park in Assam.

FIRE STAMPING RHINOS

There's a legend that if a rhinoceros sees a fire in the forest, it goes there and stamps it out. In the cult movie, *The Gods Must Be Crazy*, an African rhino puts out a campfire. But this is just a story like the one about the lady in the moon. (Don't tell me you REALLY think there is a lady in the moon!)

Rhinoceroses have also been branded as bad-tempered in stories and legends. Again, this is not true. They have bad eyesight and charge because they can't see the enemy till the enemy is really close by. However, they have very good senses of smell and hearing.

TICK BIRDS: A RHINO'S BEST FRIEND

Other than having good hearing and smell, rhinoceroses have good friends too. Tick birds are always with them and warn them of dangers. These birds are not there to tickle, but feed on the ticks on the rhino's skin. They also raise an alarm when they sense danger. In Swahili, an oxpecker, or tick bird, is called *askari wa kifaru*, which means 'the rhino's guard'. Myna, egrets and other such birds are the Indian rhino's tick birds.

SUNBURNT RHINOS

That thick, armoured skin is not as tough as it looks. Although the thick layered skin (1.5-5 cm thick) protects them from thorns and grasses, it is actually quite sensitive to sunburn and insect bites. So what do rhinos do? They wallow in mud to protect their skin!

MAGICAL RHINOS

The rhinoceros has fascinated humans since the time of the earliest civilizations. They are to be seen on the seals found in the Indus Valley civilization, too. Many believe its blood and urine have magical powers.

SOME WEIRD RHINO TRADITIONS IN INDIA AND NEPAL

• LIBATIONS OF WATER AND MILK POURED FROM A CUP MADE OUT OF RHINO HORN IS BELIEVED TO KEEP THE SOULS OF THE DEAD HAPPY.

• RHINO URINE, CONSIDERED AN ANTISEPTIC, IS HUNG FROM THE DOOR IN A VESSEL TO KEEP AWAY DISEASES AND EVIL SPIRITS.

There are other such weird beliefs in China, Burma and Thailand, too, but the main reason why rhinos are killed today is for its horns. Its horn is used for traditional medicinal and ornamental purposes. The rhino's horn's value in weight exceeds that of gold! There are numerous regular robberies of rhino horns from North American and European museums.

PESKY POACHING

Man is the rhinoceros's only natural predator. A hungry lion or crocodile may kill a sick or young rhino to eat, but man is the only animal that kills it to make use of its horn.

A kilo of rhino horn can fetch $65,000 or more. Of the five

species of rhinos, three are critically endangered–the Javan rhino, the Northern White rhino and the Sumatran rhino. A subspecies of the White rhino, the Northern White rhino has just four or fewer individuals remaining in the wild! As per an estimate in 2002, only sixty wild Javan rhinos remain in the world. The wild population of the Sumatran rhino may be less than 275. That means they may become extinct like the woolly rhino or the mammoth.

What is the most poopy method adopted by poachers to hunt a rhino?

The Indian rhino has particular places to drop its poop. So dung piles that accumulate at these places can be up to 3 feet high! A rhino, while approaching a dung pile to excrete, walks backwards. This makes it vulnerable, as it is not looking where it's headed. The mean poachers take advantage of this and lie in wait there with their traps.

THE MYSTERY OF THE FAKE HORN

All this fuss for a fake horn!

Some rhinos have one horn while others have two horns, one behind the other. However, the horn is actually a mass of compact hair! You can say it is a mass of fibre rising from the skin and is made of keratin–the same material which your nails and hair are made of. The horns grow throughout their lives, like our hair and fingernails, and re-grow if they are broken. The rhino's horn is technically 'fake' because a true horn is one which is made out of live bone at the core and only covered by keratin.

So if you're standing in a forest and an Indian rhino attacks you (since you are its only predator), it will try to slash you with its sharp incisors and canines and not with its fake horn. Since you can't outrun the rhino, just find the nearest tree to climb. And hope that the rhino at the base of the tree retreats to stamp out a jungle fire.

HORRIFYING HORN FACTS

❋ DEER DON'T HAVE HORNS, THEY HAVE ANTLERS! ANTLERS ARE BONE STRUCTURES WHICH ARE SHED AND REGROWN ANNUALLY. HORNS ARE BONES COVERED WITH A SHEATH OF KERATIN THAT KEEP GROWING FOR LIFE AND ARE NOT SHED.

❋ SOME DEER MAY NIBBLE ON THEIR OWN ANTLERS FOR CALCIUM AFTER SHEDDING THEM.

❋ A LARGE FOUR-LEGGED DINOSAUR, THE TRICERATOPS, (MEANING THREE-HORN FACE IN GREEK), HAD A LARGE BONY FRILL WITH THREE HORNS. IT SOMEWHAT RESEMBLED THE RHINOCEROS.

❋ ANOTHER DINOSAUR, THE STYRACOSAURUS (OR SPIKED LIZARD IN GREEK), HAD ONE HORN COMING OUT OF ITS NOSE, A HORN ON EACH OF ITS CHEEKS AND FOUR TO SIX HORNS FROM ITS NECK FRILL! NO WONDER THE GREEK NAMED IT 'SPIKED!'

❋ A FRENCH HORN IS NOT A FRENCH PERSON WITH A HORN, BUT A MUSICAL BRASS INSTRUMENT. ORIGINALLY, THESE MUSICAL HORNS WERE MADE OUT OF ACTUAL HORNS OF ANIMALS.

HOW DO CARACALS ATTAIN EXTRAORDINARY SPEED?

CARACALS ARE A TYPE OF CAT. THEY HELD A SPECIAL PLACE IN
ANCIENT EGYPT BECAUSE THEY WERE CONSIDERED
GUARDS OF THE DEAD PHARAOHS. SCULPTURES OF CARACALS
GUARDED THEIR TOMBS. APART FROM THIS, CARACALS
ALSO HAVE ANOTHER QUALITY—ASTONISHING SPEED.
HOW? READ ON TO FIND OUT!

WHO IS THE CARACAL?

The caracal is named after its ear, like the rhinoceros is named after its horn and the civet after its scent. The Turkish words *kara kulak* mean 'black ear'. The caracal is called siyahgosh in India. This is a Persian word—*siyah* means black and *gosh* means ear.

This black-eared caracal is a type of wild cat. And what is a cat? Cats are members of the Felidae family and include big to small cats—lions, tigers, leopards, cheetahs, lynx and caracals. Their tribe is the most perfect of all carnivores or beasts of prey because of their agility, strength, high intelligence, grace and physical characteristics that make them the perfect killers. Don't believe us? Read the following facts and decide for yourself.

FAT CAT...ER...CAT FACTS:

CLAWS

The claws, their weapons of attack, are held back by an elastic ligament. The ligament keeps them raised from the ground so they don't become blunt. These are called retractile claws. They are also protected by sheaths. The sheaths are more developed in some cats and less in others. The retractile claws emerge from the sheaths, bared in action, when they're about to strike!

SENSES

Their senses, specially of hearing and vision, are highly developed. They have the largest eyes of all carnivores. Their large upstanding ears catch the smallest sound. They can also sense with their whiskers and feel with the whisker-like bristles on their forearms (forearm in a four-legged animal is part of the foreleg between the elbow and the knee).

FEET

Their strong feet help them seize prey in a lightning rush or leap. While stalking, they walk on their toes to keep their approach stealthy and silent. Many cats like the tiger place their hind feet exactly where they'd placed their forefeet in order to make their approach soundless. If you see their track, it'll look like that of a biped (one that has two feet).

TEETH

The great cats have large fangs like canines! These are much longer than their other teeth. When their jaws are closed, the canines are interlocked and when the jaws open, the canines can penetrate the prey, seize it, hold it and kill it!

COLOURATION

The colour of their coat also helps them camouflage themselves in their surrounding—be it mountains, savannahs, grasslands, plains or jungles. Their tawny colours and markings differ from species to species, and even within the same species in different regions. In the Arctic they have a lesser tendency for bright colours and the colours darken and enrich with increase in temperature and humidity in their environment.

TONGUE

Did you think that the tongue was only for tasting? Yours is... not theirs! Cats have a rough, raspy tongue. It is like a scraping paper with which they can lick clean the meat clinging to the bones of their kill. Their tongue can stick to your finger like pins!

So that's a cat for you—the topmost predator in the food chain. The role of each creature in the food chain is very clearly defined. There are carnivores that eat animals, herbivores that eat vegetable matter, omnivores that eat both, scavengers that eat the dead and parasites that survive on the living. Sometimes, carnivores eat the dead and scavengers hunt.

THE KARAKULAK OR SIYAHGOSH

The caracal is a wild cat with tufted ears that are black at the back. With its tufted ears and long hind legs, it looks like a lynx and is also called a 'desert lynx' too. But it is not a lynx as it is smaller in build, has no ruff of hair around its face and has a longer tail. It is more closely related to the serval and the African Golden Cat.

Caracals live in a variety of habitats from semi-desert areas to grasslands and thick forests. But it prefers semi-desert areas and scrub jungles. Although it is found widely in Asia and Africa, it is rare in India and fast approaching extinction. Humans hunt them for their fur and because they kill their livestock.

Like your home is your territory (sorry, only your room is your territory), caracals also have their own territories. Theirs are spread over dozens of kilometres! They generally live alone or in pairs while mating. They mark their territory by leaving their faeces in visible locations and spraying their urine on bushes and logs.

Caracals don't have a pattern on their coat, except some light spots on their underside. Their coat is tawny grey or reddish in colour or the colour of sand. Those found in dry regions are paler in colour than their woodland dwelling cousins.

EGYPTIAN CARACALS

In ancient Egypt, cats, including caracals, were given special significance. There are wall paintings of caracals in tombs and their sculptures guarded the tombs of pharaohs.

Egyptians had mastered the art of embalming dead bodies and they did it with cats too! Many mummies made out of cats, including caracals, have been found.

CAT AMONG THE PIGEONS

I bet you're thinking, 'Why on earth is this chapter named "How Do Caracals Attain Extraordinary Speed?"' Don't fume, we'll tell you why.

Caracals have extraordinary agility. They are amazing acrobats due to their perfect accord of eyes and feet and long hind legs. Historically, they were kept as pets in India and Iran. They can be easily trained like the cheetah, which was also tamed in the olden days for hunting small deer, hare, foxes and birds like pigeons, cranes and peafowls.

Caracals were champion performers of a sport that was once popular in Iran and India–*pigeon killing*! A caracal would be set loose on a flock of pigeons. Onlookers watching the sport would make bets on how many birds it could take down. A star performer could leap and knock out nine to ten birds before they could even leave the ground, before you could say, 'Youmustbekiddingme!' Where do you think the phrase 'to put the cat among the pigeons' came from?

When we talk of super speed, most of us only refer to the cheetah, the fastest animal on earth. Now we know that there's another creature called the siyahgosh or the caracal that can dart super-fast. But its fast speed has not been good enough to protect it from greedy humans. The only thing it's fast approaching in India is extinction. Like the cheetah, it might soon be extinct from India.

If we guard the caracal like it guards the ancient Egyptian tombs, we may still be able to save it. There is a lot of effort going on towards saving the tiger, but not a fraction of it goes towards saving the caracal, which is left in much smaller pockets in India than the tiger. Next time someone talks about saving the tiger, you can talk about saving the caracal too.

FUNNY FASTEST ANIMAL FACTS

* THE PEREGRINE FALCON IS THE FASTEST BIRD. IN FACT, IT'S THE FASTEST CREATURE IN THE ANIMAL KINGDOM. IT CAN ACHIEVE A SPEED OF 389 KM/HR WHEN IT DIVES DOWN TO HUNT!

* THE GAME FISH BLACK MARLIN CAN ATTAIN A SPEED OF 130 KM/HR!

* THE FREE-TAILED BAT CAN FLY AT A SPEED OF 96.6 KM/HR!

* THE AMERICAN ANTELOPE IS THE FASTEST ANIMAL OVER LONG DISTANCES AND CAN RUN AT A SPEED OF 88.5 KM/HR!

* THE HIGHEST SPEED ATTAINED BY A HUMAN IS ONLY 44.72 KM/HR.

WHY DO FIREFLIES GLOW?

IMAGINE YOU HAD A REAR END THAT LIT UP! THAT WOULD MAKE
YOU THE BUTT OF ALL JOKES, WOULDN'T IT? BUT NOT THE FIREFLY.
FIREFLIES OR LIGHTNING BUGS ARE NOT THE SUBJECT OF JOKES
BUT OF STUDY, DUE TO THEIR GLOWING ABDOMENS.

IS IT REALLY MAGICAL, YOU MAY WONDER. WELL, THEN FIRST WE
NEED TO UNDERSTAND WHAT MAGIC IS. THE POTION THAT THE
WITCH GIVES YOU TO TURN THE CLASS BULLY'S FACE GREEN CAN
JUST BE A POTENT HERBAL MIXTURE. THE FLYING CARPET
MIGHT HAVE A PROPELLER AT THE BASE. THE ROBE THAT MAKES
YOU INVISIBLE MAY JUST BE A LIE! AND IN THE FIREFLY'S CASE,
THE MAGIC IS CHEMICAL.

SPOOKY BIOLUMINESCENCE

Ancient sailors used to see fireflies on the passing shores
and mistook them for twinkling fairies. We might too, if we didn't
know how fireflies glow.

The chemical reaction through which a firefly produces light
is called bioluminescence. It occurs in the firefly's lower abdomen.
This is a 'cold light' not a 'hot light'. Light emitted when things get
hot is called incandescence—like the light from a bulb. Hot light
would burn the fireflies' insides!

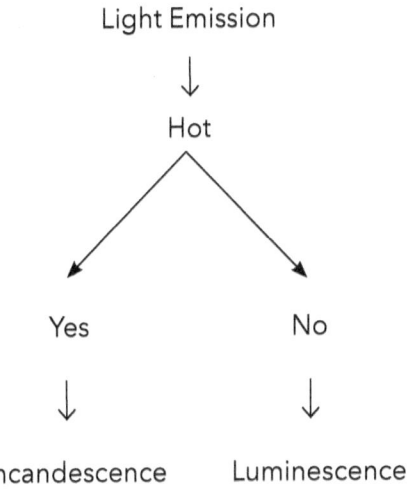

Light Emission

↓

Hot

Yes   No

↓   ↓

Incandescence   Luminescence

Cold light produced by *living* creatures is called bioluminescence.

FIREFLIES ARE FOUND ON ALL CONTINENTS EXCEPT THE ANTARCTIC. THEY LOVE WARM AND HUMID WEATHER AND COME OUT IN SUMMERS. TWO THOUSAND KNOWN SPECIES OF FIREFLIES TWINKLE ACROSS THE GLOBE. FIREFLIES ARE THE MOST COMMON CREATURES WITH BIOLUMINESCENCE ON LAND. BUT THIS PHENOMENON IS FOUND MORE WIDELY IN THE SEA. THERE ARE MANY FUNGI, FISH AND OTHER MARINE CREATURES THAT GLOW! THEY GLOW PALE-RED, YELLOW OR GREEN AND IT WOULD INDEED BE A MAGICAL EXPERIENCE TO SEE THE GLOWING CREATURES IN THE DARK DEPTHS OF AN OCEAN.

WOW! HOW?
Turn over to find out how fireflies glow!

These little twinkling fireflies are incredibly useful. Scientists wanted to know if animal genes could be transferred to plants. In 1986, they inserted the firefly's genes in a tobacco plant and successfully made a glowing tobacco plant!

Some spacecraft missions like the ones sent to study and look for life on Mars are fitted with the chemical luciferase. If ATP can be detected, there is a fair possibility of life existing in outer space. Firefly luciferase is used in medical studies such as reporter genes– a gene that is attached to another gene to follow its sequence and activity–to better understand certain disease like cancer. The luciferase, due to its ability to glow, makes a good reporter.

Fireflies are not only of use to scientists, but also to artists. Experts wonder if the famous Italian artist Caravaggio prepared his canvases with the powder of dried fireflies. He did that to create a light-sensitive surface, on which he projected the image to be painted.

WHY, FIREFLY?

Why do fireflies glow? Not to remind the ancient mariners of fairy tales, for sure.

THEY COMMUNICATE THROUGH FLASHES AND STEADY GLOWS, MOSTLY TO ATTRACT A MATE. DIFFERENT SPECIES HAVE DIFFERENT FLASH PATTERNS AND WAVELENGTHS TO COMMUNICATE. (NOW YOU KNOW WHY THEY SAY YOUR WAVELENGTHS SHOULD MATCH!) IN CERTAIN SPECIES, THE FEMALES DON'T FLY, BUT RESPOND TO THE FLASHY MALES THROUGH LIGHT SIGNALS. SOME SPECIES EVEN HAVE SIMILAR FLASH PATTERNS BUT FLY AT DIFFERENT HEIGHTS TO AVOID CONFUSION.

Some fireflies that fly during the day do not produce light but communicate through pheromones. These are chemicals usually produced by animals and insects to attract a mate.

Some fireflies, especially in tropical regions, synchronize their flash sequences in large groups. The reason most likely could be social behaviour or diet. But who knows, it could be attitude as well!

That's not all. Female *Photuris* fireflies mimic flashes of other species. Why do they do that? To lure the males of other species and then eat them, of course.

GORGEOUS GLOW-WORMS

Not just the firefly larvae, but even their eggs glow! So the larvae are called glow-worms. (In America and Europe, glow-worms also refer to the larvae of different kinds of beetles.) Fireflies lay their eggs in damp soil near riverbeds and marshes, just below the surface. When the larvae or glow-worms come out, they have plenty to eat. These worms are not just cosy glowing cuties but also specialized predators. They prey on snails, slugs and even other larvae! Some have special grooved mandibles—a pair of cutting, crushing, tooth-like extensions near the mouth—that put the digestive juices directly on the prey!

Glow-worms hibernate during winter. Some may sleep not just for a season but for years! They sleep underground or under barks of trees. Once they're awake, they get back to feeding. After eating for many weeks, they go inside a mud house to become a pupa. When they emerge from the pupa, they've been transformed into fireflies with glowing bellies! Adult fireflies don't eat much. Some may hunt while many others don't eat at all. If they do, they eat only pollen, nectar or dew. The adult firefly lives only for a few days.

EXTINGUISHING FIREFLIES

We've cut down jungles, filled marshes and pools to make our houses, thrown our garbage into clean streams, made the air smelly with pollution from our cars, air-conditioners and what-not. As a result, fireflies have no place to live, so they die. The pesticides that we use in the farms also kill them.

Fireflies are quite sensitive to light and even moonlit nights are too bright for them. The bright lights in cities dazzle so much that the tiny twinkles of the poor fireflies are lost in them. If they can't signal to each other, they can't mate and can't grow in numbers. You can help fireflies by not switching on too many lights in your garden at night.

At places where there are lots of fireflies, kids and grown-ups often catch them in jars to keep overnight or take out on a picnic or a garden barbeque. But they should be released in the morning again. Unfortunately, in many places, fireflies have just vanished and people have forgotten all about them.

PRAY I'M NOT YOUR PREY

In nature, generally animals—both the hunter and the hunted—try to hide themselves by blending into their surroundings with the colours on their skin or fur. But there are a few animals that don't hide but display their presence through bright colours. These bold animals usually have a defence mechanism like poison or a nauseous stink. The hunter, who has once had a bad experience, tries to avoid them later.

Fireflies don't have warning colours, but a warning light! They taste terrible and some are even poisonous to eat. So the fireflies use their cold fire to speak to their mates, attract unsuspecting prey, warn predators, and look grand in the process! We certainly can't do all that. Hmmm…now that we think about it, maybe they *are* little fairies whom we mistake for glowing bugs.

GREAT GLOWING CREATURES FACTS

※ THE DELICATE LOOKING, ALMOST TRANSPARENT JELLYFISH DEVOURS OTHER JELLYFISH AND EMITS A GREEN-BLUE GLOW.

※ THE GHOST FUNGUS, A GILLED MUSHROOM, IS POISONOUS TO EAT BUT GLOWS MAGNIFICENTLY IN THE DARK.

※ THE FIREFLY SQUID, FOUND IN THE WESTERN PACIFIC OCEAN, SPARKLES TO ATTRACT SMALL FISH.

❋ THE ANGRY LOOKING DEEP SEA ANGLER FISH HAS A FLESHY LUMINOUS GROWTH ON THE HEAD, WHICH ACTS AS A LURE AND GIVES IT ITS NAME.

❋ DINOFLAGELLATE, SINGLE-CELLED MARINE FLOATING ORGANISMS, INCLUDE VARIETIES THAT GLOW IN THE WATER.

WHY DOES THE SLOTH BEAR HUG?

IS THE SLOTH BEAR—SHAGGY, UNKEMPT AND RECLUSIVE—REALLY A
ROMANTIC? WEARING A DARK COAT OF HAIR, WALKING
SOMETIMES ON FOURS AND AT OTHER TIMES ON
TWO LEGS, SWAYING IN ITS SLOW, FLAPPING GAIT, DOES MR SLOTH
BEAR HUG HUMANS? LET'S INVESTIGATE IF
THIS ROMANTIC TALE IS FACT OR FICTION.

THE BEAR HUG

Let's first examine the traits of bears by analysing their anatomy, nature and behaviour.

A bear has three major weaknesses:

Weak eyesight

Weak hearing

Clumsiness

And to top all that, it sleeps deeply.

Picture a sloth bear, short of sight and hearing, sleeping like a log under a jutting rock. Now you are walking in the forest, whistling a tune. In such a situation, you suddenly become aware of a sleeping bear ahead, or the bear becomes aware of you. The bear gets up, wobbly and stunned from sleep, probably on two legs. (Remember, if you come across a big animal in the wild, it might try to stand on two legs if it can, or jump on you, so that it can reach your vital organs. It'll try to bring you down to the ground and then fight you. Also, generally speaking, animals attack in a clockwise direction.)

But it is not you who goes into the forest walking alone, whistling a tune. It is the village women, though they don't idly whistle a tune. They go to the jungles to collect wood for firewood and cut grass for fodder. Sometimes, these women are engrossed in work and are unaware of the presence of a sleeping bear and wander too close to it. When the bear is rudely woken up from its deep sleep, it stands on two feet and tries to push its victim down with its front legs, or hold the victim down with its front limbs, which looks like an embrace. It paws the face and chest of the victim with its long nails in a hugging motion. This can inflict the most terrible wounds.

If you're standing at a distance and seeing the bear attack, it might seem that the bear is hugging the woman. Because of its dense coat of hair, you can't see the contraction of its muscles or the fierce expression in its small eyes. The attack can be mistaken for a clumsy romantic gesture by a roly-poly bear. That's the reason why hunters, tribals and villagers feel that the sloth bear is 'romantic'.

A SLOTH BEAR IS THE MOST UNPREDICTABLE OF WILD ANIMALS AND MAY ATTACK UNPROVOKED. THOSE WHO SURVIVE BEAR ATTACKS ARE OFTEN LEFT WITH TERRIBLY DISFIGURED HEADS AND FACES. NOT QUITE SO ROMANTIC NOW, EH? AND IT'S NOT JUST HUNTERS, TRIBALS AND VILLAGERS WHO BELIEVE THE BEAR TO BE 'ROMANTIC'. DON'T WE ALL USE THE EXPRESSION 'BEAR HUG'? NONE OF US WOULD LIKE TO GET THE ACTUAL ONE, THOUGH!

SLOTHY STORY

In the olden days, when sloth bears were hunted, there was another story that did the rounds. A sloth bear never leaves its wounded mate and always carries the injured to safety. So the animal is not just romantic, it's loyal and heroic too. Now let's analyse this story also.

Since the sloth bear's senses are weak, when one of the two bears roaming in a jungle is injured, the other cannot quickly understand what happened. It thinks that its companion is being mischievous. It doesn't take much to annoy the haughty sloth bear. It becomes cross and attacks its own mate aggressively, screaming at the top of its voice.

The hunter, who is standing at a distance, sees the ferociousness and hears the roars, and may get a different impression. It might seem to him that the bear is distressed and is trying to help its mate. Here again, the bear's long, shaggy coat and plump body hide the reality and mislead the observer.

THOUGH ITS HEARING AND SIGHT ARE NOT VERY GOOD, THE SLOTH BEAR'S SENSE OF SMELL IS STRONG. AND EVEN THESE SENSES VARY IN DIFFERENT KINDS OF BEARS. THE HIMALAYAN BLACK BEAR CAN HEAR AND SEE BETTER THAN THE BROWN BEAR. THE BROWN BEAR HAS A KEENER SENSE OF SMELL THAN THE SLOTH BEAR AND CAN SMELL THE WIND-BORNE SCENT OF A MAN FROM A MILE AWAY! ALTHOUGH THEIR FACULTIES ARE WEAK, BEARS HAVE TRADITIONALLY BEEN TRAINED BY HUMANS AND HAVE BEEN STAR PERFORMERS IN CIRCUSES AS WELL AS STREET SHOWS.

THE GREAT BIG BEAR QUIZ

Although the sloth bear is neither romantic nor heroic, it is an awfully interesting animal. It has a black coat with a V-shaped white mark on the chest. It walks with a slow, shuffling gait, placing its feet in a flapping motion.

Let's find out more about the not-so-romantic sloth bear:

(1) What is the sloth bear's favourite food?
    (a) Wild Figs
    (b) Honey
    (c) Termites

(2) What does a bear use to trace a termite's mound?
    (a) Nose
    (b) Eyes
    (c) Hands

(3) Who eats 'bear's bread'?
    (a) Bear cubs
    (b) Humans
    (c) Both

(4) What does a sloth bear do best?
    (a) Climb
    (b) Swim
    (c) Both

(5) Who hunts bears?
    (a) Tiger
    (b) Man
    (c) Both

(6) Bruno, the pet bear of Kenneth Anderson's wife, ate many things including…
    (a) Plastic Cups
    (b) Motor Oil
    (c) Books

ANSWERS:

Ans. 1 Honey! *Bhalu* or the sloth bear mainly eats fruits and insects. It wanders alone at night looking for grub. In summers, it gorges on wood apple, jujube or Indian plum, jackfruit, mangoes, wild figs and fruits of the banyan tree. It climbs up trees for fruits and shakes them down. Like a few other animals, it also enjoys chewing on the petals of the mahua tree. Mahua is a tropical tree with a lot of uses. Its leaves are eaten by a kind of moth that produces tussar silk, skin care products are made of the sap derived from the tree, its flowers are used by tribals to prepare medicine and even fermented to make a local alcohol called Mahuwa.

In monsoons, the sloth bear feasts more on insects and looks for them under rocks, in tree crevices, fallen logs and barks. Its main insect food is termite. If you see a destroyed termite mound, it is safe to guess that a bear is about. A bear living around human settlements may raid on maize, sugarcanes and drink toddy. But honey remains its most favourite food. It knocks down honeycombs to get to the honey and the poor angry bees can do little to attack the bear through its shaggy coat.

Ans. 2 Nose. Bears and dogs have common ancestors—so they both sniff! Once it has located a termite mound, the bear uses its long sickle-shaped claws to break it. It reaches the large combs at the bottom and blows away the dirt, puffing loudly. The special muzzle and lower lip of a sloth bear is like a vacuum nozzle—the terminator of termites. The bear nosily sucks in the insects and you can hear it do so from a distance in the jungle.

Ans. 3 Both. Since sloth bears are extremely fond of honey, they feed it to their cubs too. The mamma bear (a female bear is called a sow and a male is called a boar) eats the honeycomb first. She also eats fruits like jackfruits and wood apple. While feeding the cubs, she regurgitates a sticky mixture of half-digested fruits and honeycomb. That's called 'bear's bread'. It hardens into a dark yellow bread-like mass. Not just the cubs, but even some humans consider it a delicacy!

Ans. 4 Both. Yes, yes, they are clumsy and fat, but they are very good climbers! Not only can they climb trees (were you thinking of climbing a tree to escape a sloth bear?) but can also hang upside down like sloths! They love water as well and mainly go into it to play. Sloth bears need a constant water supply and travel long distances to get water in the summers. If they find a dry water bed, they dig in with their claws to reach the water.

Ans. 5 Both. The sloth bear is too powerful to be hunted down by predators. They generally leave this bad-tempered chap alone although a pack of wild dogs or wolves may attack it. Generally panthers and bears avoid each other in the forest, though tigers may hunt sloth bears at times. The easiest thing for the tiger to do is wait near a termite mound and pounce on the bear. If the bear sees the tiger, it charges at the tiger, crying loudly. The tiger usually tries to avoid the confrontation and the vicious claw wounds, so it retreats.

The only major predator of the bear is man, who hunts it for use in medicines because he thinks this can cure his diseases. Pah…tall story! Scores of bears are illegally hunted, their bile exported to Japan and other countries, their paws, teeth and body parts slashed and used to prepare medicines and food delicacies.

Ans. 6 Motor oil! She kept an an orphaned bear cub as a pet. He was an affectionate bear and knew various tricks like pointing a bamboo stick like a gun and holding a wood block like a baby. British officers in India often kept sloth bears as pets as they could be tamed easily. Since the pre-Mughal era, bears have been trained as performers. Kalandars captured and trained bears in dancing and performed in the Mughal courts. Even a couple of decades ago, it was not an unusual site to see a dancing bear with its kalandar on the streets of India.

Sloth bears may not be romantic, but they're great performers, swimmers, climbers and pretty savage when they want to be. When you want to hug, hug your teddy, and when you see a sloth bear in the forest, *run*!

BEWITCHING BEAR FACTS

❋ THE TEDDY BEAR TOY IS NAMED AFTER THE US PRESIDENT THEODORE ROOSEVELT WHO WAS ALSO REFERRED TO AS 'TEDDY'. DURING A HUNTING TRIP IN MISSISSIPPI, A BEAR WAS CLUBBED AND TIED TO A TREE FOR PRESIDENT ROOSEVELT TO SHOOT. HE REFUSED SAYING IT WAS UNSPORTSMANLIKE AND ORDERED THE BEAR TO BE PUT OUT OF ITS MISERY. TOYMAKERS, INSPIRED FROM THE CARTOONS IN THE NEWSPAPERS, DEVELOPED A SOFT TOY CALLED 'TEDDY BEAR', WHICH WAS AN INSTANT HIT!

❋ AFRICA, WHICH HAS A GREAT VARIETY OF ANIMALS, DOESN'T HAVE ANY BEARS.

❋ THE NANDI BEAR IS A LEGENDARY, GIANT, HYENA-LIKE ANIMAL SUPPOSED TO LIVE IN AFRICA, LIKE THE ABOMINABLE SNOWMAN IS SUPPOSED TO LIVE IN THE HIMALAYAS.

❋ GRIZZLY BEARS HAVE EXCELLENT MEMORIES.

❋ POLAR BEARS ARE SOCIAL ANIMALS AND HAVE OFTEN BEEN SEEN PLAYING WITH SLEDGE DOGS.

WHY DOES THE CIVET CARRY A POUCH OF FOUL-SMELLING LIQUID?

WHAT IF YOU HAD A POUCH AT YOUR REAR END? A POUCH WITH LIPS THAT OPENED AND WAS FULL OF FOUL-SMELLING LIQUID. EVERY TIME THE CLASS MONITOR CAME TO COLLECT YOUR HOMEWORK OR A TEACHER GAVE YOU A SCOLDING OR THE SCHOOL BULLY ATE YOUR LUNCH (OH, DID YOU SAY YOU'RE THE BULLY YOURSELF?) OR YOUR MUM RUFFLED YOUR STYLISH HAIR, YOU COULD JUST OPEN THAT POUCH AND SQUIRT SOME YUCKY-SMELLING LIQUID ON YOUR PREDATOR! WOULDN'T YOU LIKE THAT? WELL, OKAY, PERHAPS NOT WITH THE POUCH LOCATED AT THE REAR END, BUT SOME OTHER PLACE MAYBE.

CIVETS HAVE THIS COOL, SECRET MECHANISM. ONCE YOU FIND OUT WHAT IT IS, YOU MUST KEEP IT HUSH-HUSH, SO THAT ITS CUNNING PREDATORS DON'T GET A *WHIFF* OF IT!

WHAT IS A CIVET?

A civet is a small mammal, similar to a cat, yet different. It lives mainly in the tropics of Asia and Africa but most civet species are found in Southeast Asia. A civet has a long body, short stumpy legs, an elongated head and a pointed muzzle. Its favourite habitat is tropical rainforests, but it is also found in woodlands, grasslands and mountains (up to a height of 7,000 feet).

Bear cats, palm civets, linsangs and over a dozen or so mammals belong to the family Viverridae–close relatives to the family Felidae (cats).

The Viverridae family tree dates back 50 million years. They lived in the tropical forests of the Old World. Scientists have discovered fossils of true civets from southern India dating back to prehistoric times.

Civets are mainly active at night, and either hunt or eat vegetable matter unlike cats, who live wholly by hunting. They eat anything from fruits, snakes and insects to roots, small birds, lizards, berries and mice. Some palette!

One of the senses that they use is mobile. What is it?

(a) Ears
(b) Nose
(c) Whiskers
(d) Toes

Ans. Whiskers! Civets have mobile whiskers. (And of course their toes are mobile as well. They walk on them, don't they?) They can move their whiskers backwards and forwards. A Himalayan Palm Civet in captivity always touched its food with its whiskers before it ate it. Civets also have a sharp sense of smell, eyesight and hearing, which they utilize while hunting or looking for vegetable matter.

ARE YOU A NIGHT ANIMAL?

There are two kinds of animals depending on when they are out and about–night animals and day animals (nocturnal and diurnal). This is why two animals living in the same area sometimes never meet! Imagine your elder brother is a night animal. By the time you wake up, he's asleep and when you go to bed he's awake.

The set of hunters and hunted are different during the day and during the night and make up distinct food chains. Then there are predators and prey that feed both by day and night or during dawn or dusk. Some night animals may even come out on a cloudy day to feed. But largely, the day and night animals are different and maintain different food chains. As you go towards the colder, temperate regions, the night animals become fewer in number till you reach the Poles, where there are no night animals at all.

Most civets are night animals. Their claws and hairless soles aid them in leading a semi-arboreal lifestyle and help them hunt both on trees and on ground.

The toddy cat (or the Common Palm Civet) sleeps curled up in the hollow of mango or palm trees during the daytime. During the fruiting season, it hangs around coffee and pineapple plantations. In the areas where toddy is tapped from the palm trees, the toddy cat climbs up the trees during the night and steals the sweet juice collected in pots. After drinking the liquid, it may even curl up and sleep on the tree during the day. Toddy cats are easily tamed and are even friendly and playful.

In the olden days, Greeks kept genets, a kind of civet found in southern Europe and Africa, as a domestic cat.

The bear-faced bear-cat (binturong) gets up at dusk and goes out to find food. Its tail, strong and muscular at the base, is prehensile and also hairy. It tucks its head under its bushy tail to sleep tight in the daytime. At night, it uses its tail to climb down trees by anchoring it on branches!

CIVET COFFEE

Oh yes, there is a civet coffee! Berries are a favourite food of civets, especially coffee berries. When the berries ripen, civets come to coffee plantations and gorge on them.

Once the berry season is over, they go away and their poop is collected by men. The civets digest the berries but pass the coffee beans, processed with their stomach enzymes, with their poop. These beans are gathered, cleaned and used to make a special type of rare coffee called civet coffee. Although civet coffee is harvested in countries like Philippines, Indonesia, Vietnam and India, only around 450 kg is produced every year and can cost around $100 per cup!

SCENT AND STINK

So you thought stinking isn't cool. Well, think twice. Almost all civets possess anal stink glands. What do they have it for? To communicate and to drive away their predators.

COMMUNICATION

The little ones of the Small Indian Civet, which can be easily tamed, make a loud and piercing cat-like meow and the adults make a tick-tick like clicking sound when happy. But most of these civets don't give out calls or communicate vocally with each other much except the bear-cat which growls and howls loudly.

Civets generally leave a trail of their scent glands, marking their territories with it and communicate with each other through their scent.

Both males and females have these glands located beneath their tails. The shape and structure of these glands is different in different civets. In some civets you can even see this pouch externally. It is a fairly large pouch with thick hairy lips which open and close. Others just have a fold of skin through which the glands discharge the secretion.

DEFENCE

Civets are both the hunter and the hunted. They feed on smaller animals and become prey to the larger ones. Their teeth and claws, which are helpful in hunting, are of course smaller than their predators. So what do they do? They stink!

When cornered, civets tend to squirt a vile-smelling yellow fluid from their anal glands to daze the predator. The discharge is so repugnant and strong that the attacker is blinded for the moment or nauseated and disoriented by the smell. The civet takes advantage of this and runs to safety.

Now if you had this kind of defence mechanism, would you hide it or boast about it? Guess it would be the latter. And that's what the civet does.

MASK FOR A TASK

Unlike other animals which have camouflage colourings to hide themselves, the ones which have weapons of nauseous odour advertise their presence through their colouration.

It is believed that once a predator attacks the animal and experiences its deadly stink, it associates other fellows of the species with their bold display of colours and pattern. In future, it tries to avoid having them for a meal. Stink bugs and blister beetles that are coloured a bright red, yellow and black follow a similar tactic.

MAMMALS WITH STINK GLANDS LIKE POLECATS, SKUNKS AND CIVETS, DON'T HAVE SUCH BRIGHT ATTIRES LIKE THE STINKY BUGS AND BEETLES. THEY'RE MUCH BIGGER THAN THE BUGS AND DON'T WANT TO LOOK SO FANCY. THEY HAVE A LESS EYE-CATCHING COLOURATION. THESE ANIMALS, WHO DON'T WANT TO BE PAINTED IN DANDY COLOURS, WARN THE ENEMIES BY A DISPLAY. THEY HAVE BLACK AND WHITE, OR DARK AND LIGHT 'MASKED' FACES. THAT'S WAY COOLER-LIKE BANDITS, OR BATMAN.

When these mammals are in danger, they make their dark hair stand erect. The hair is in contrast to their light under-fur and makes the animals look bold, brash and a bit frightening.

The predators remember it and try to avoid the foul-smelling creatures later on.

THE CIVET OF THE CIVET

If men can drink coffee processed from the civet's poop, surely they can't have any issues using the secretion from the civet's anal glands! The word civet is derived from the Arabic word *zabat*, a term given to the scent derived from these glands. The African civet is the best known civet species from which humans historically collected this musky secretion. Musk is an aromatic substance used to prepare perfumes. It is obtained from the glands of a few animals like the musk deer, the African civet, the musk turtle and even the musk beetle! But nowadays, due to the decreasing number of these animals and the wacky methods used to obtain their glandular secretions, companies are making synthetic musk.

The musk derived from the civet is also called civet.

Civet is one of the most expensive essential oils in the world, used for making perfumes. It is also used to flavour tobacco.

There are two methods to get this oil from a civet's anal glands:

1. Kill the animal and remove the pouch
2. Scrape the secretion from the live animal's pouch

Although you get a fat amount of money for bringing in the pouch of a freshly killed animal, the usual method is to scrape the secretion out of a live civet.

Another awesome quality of the civets is that they are great ratters. When they live near human civilization, they do a great service by eating swarms of these vermin. The Black Death, one of the most horrific pandemics in human history, was caused by mice and killed around 200 million people! This plague is said to have spread widely through the fleas living on black mice that used to travel in merchant ships on the Mediterranean sea and into Europe.

But civets are decreasing in number and the rat population is growing more and more. We're destroying their homes and many civets like the otter civet have now become rare and endangered. If they become extinct it'll be our great loss. After all, where will we find a scent-maker, coffee processor, pet and ratter all rolled into one? Not in our nearest supermarket for sure.

DEADLY ANIMAL DEFENCE FACTS

※ THE BOMBARDIER BEETLE EXPLODES A 100 DEGREE CENTIGRADE TOXIC SPRAY FROM ITS ABDOMEN AT ITS PREDATOR!

※ MANY KINDS OF SLUG CATERPILLARS HAVE STINGING, NEEDLE-LIKE SPINES ALONG THEIR BACK! FANCY EATING ONE SUCH SLUG.

※ THE TEXAS HORNED LIZARD CAN SHOOT SQUIRTS OF BLOODS FROM ITS EYES ON THE UNSUSPECTING HUNTER!

※ THE HAGFISH HAS SLIME GLANDS WHICH CAN SECRETE MUCUS IN WATER, CLOGGING THE GILLS OF THE PREDATOR!

※ AS A PREDATOR APPROACHES A WHITE-TAILED DEER FAWN, IT PRETENDS TO BE DEAD—NOT JUST BY LYING STILL ON THE GROUND, BUT BY REDUCING ITS HEART RATE FROM 155 TO ONLY 38 BEATS PER MINUTE!

WHY DO SCORPIONS LIVE TOGETHER ON THE SCORPION HILL IN RAJASTHAN?

THERE EXISTS, IN THE PANARWA JUNGLES OF UDAIPUR DISTRICT, RAJASTHAN, A HILLOCK WHERE THOUSANDS OF SCORPIONS LIVE TOGETHER. THIS HILLOCK IS AROUND 100 METRES HIGH AND SITUATED AROUND 240 KM FROM UDAIPUR. 'SO WHAT?' YOU ASK. THE HILLOCK IS UNUSUAL BECAUSE IT IS BELIEVED THAT SCORPIONS GENERALLY LIVE ALONE AND NOT IN A COMMUNITY. 'WHY NOT?' YOU ASK AGAIN. WELL, THAT'S THE QUESTION. WHY AREN'T SCORPIONS SOCIAL? IF THEY'RE NOT, WHY HAVE THEY COME TOGETHER AT THE SCORPION HILL?

WHO WAS SERKET?

Serket was the Egyptian goddess of healing poisonous stings and the protector of the dead, who carried a scorpion on her head. She was an important goddess as some of the most dangerous scorpions in the world reside in North Africa and their sting can kill. In fact, two early Egyptian kings were called 'Scorpion Kings'. Historians are still wondering why they were called so; maybe it was just to project a tough image.

If a scorpion can be so deadly that the Egyptians needed a goddess for it, imagine what a whole colony of scorpions can do!

Let's see what a scorpion is and why it is feared and also revered.

SCARY SCORPIONS

The word scorpion is derived from the Greek word *skorpíos*. But they're not just found in Greece. They're found all over the world, except in Antarctica.

What can be so scary about an insect? Well, the scorpion is not an insect. It is an arachnid. What's the difference? Arthropods (meaning animals with jointed legs) are invertebrate animals that include:

- insects (like mosquitoes, wasps, bugs)
- crustaceans (like crabs, lobsters)
- arachnids (like spiders, scorpions)

So the spider is not an insect and nor is the scorpion. While insects have three pairs of legs, arachnids have four. And do you know how many eyes scorpions have? Up to twelve! Two on the head and two to five pairs on the side of the head. In spite of so many eyes, they still can't see clearly and use their highly sensitive hair to sense, and even taste, objects.

The body of a scorpion is divided into three parts: head, abdomen and tail. A scorpion's tail is divided into six segments and curves over its head. The sixth segment bears the telson–the poisonous sting! The telson is used both on preys and predators, and also on all those teasing the scorpion.

They also have claws or pincers on their mouth, like crabs. After all, they're more closely related to a horseshoe crab than to an insect.

TERRIFYING SCORPION FACTS

- Scorpions 'moult' like snakes. Snakes remove their outer skin periodically, while scorpions shed their outer case (or exoskeleton). The young ones may do that five to seven times a year. When these tough guys are without their outer skeleton, they are not that tough. So they go in hiding to avoid attackers till the time their armour grows back again. Animals moult for a number of reasons: for growing or shedding their winter coats, to change to breeding colours, to get rid of damaged feathers and so on. Scorpions remove their entire exoskeleton when they outgrow it, like snakes remove their entire outer skin.

- Scorpions are believed to be the first animals that moved from water to land. Millions of years ago, scorpions lived in shallow tropical seas and had gills instead of lungs. But these creatures soon decided that sea was not cool enough for them and came out on land. And what is more, they have not changed much in these millions of years, as their fossils show.

- Scorpions are survivors because they are incredibly tough! Their survival skills have helped them live in the harshest environments on earth. Some species, if they don't find food, can live on one meal a year! They can reduce their metabolic rate in order to do so. Scientists have even stored scorpions in a freezer overnight. The next day, when they were brought out, they just defrosted and started to walk again!

- Scorpions glow under ultraviolet light! Once scientists discovered the ability of scorpions to glow under UV light, they took out their handheld lamps and went out for night surveys of these creatures. Scorpions became much easier to spot as they are nocturnal and active at night. Naturalists discovered scores of new species of scorpions after that.

- Buthidae are the most dangerous of all scorpions. The deathstalker is one of them. Out of the 1,700+ species of scorpions found all over the world, only about twenty-five are fatal enough to kill a human with their venom. Their deadly reputation is a bit overhyped.

- If you take a normal lamp or torch (not UV) and throw the light on a scorpion, it will go here and there and try to evade it. Scorpions are photophobic, i.e. they don't like light. They don't want to be seen by hungry mice, lizards or birds who feast on them. That is why you'll find them most of the time hiding in shoes, under bedcovers, stones, dead wood, dry dung pellets and in crevices and other such dark places, including their burrows. So if you are out camping in the wilderness, always whack your shoes before wearing them. Same goes for your bedsheets/blankets/mats.

- In China, snake and scorpion wines are used as pain relievers and antidotes. One look at that wine bottle with a snake or a scorpion inside it will make you so numb that you won't be able to feel any pain! Great pain relievers!

- All scorpions are carnivores. They generally kill small arthropods. Bigger scorpions can also kill lizards and mice.

- As soon as an insect touches the highly sensitive hair on the scorpion's claws or pincers, it grabs the prey, whips its telson and stings it. Some scorpions have deadlier venom and others stronger claws. Depending on that, they either crush the prey and kill it or paralyse it with the venom.

- Scorpions have external digestion. Once the prey is dead or paralysed, small claw-like gears come out of their mouth to pull in small bits of the tasty insect or lizard or whatever it's having for dinner. These small bits are sent to the pre-oral cavity below these claw-like gears or chelicerae. Scorpions can consume only liquid. Now lizards, mice and insects don't come in liquid form.

So scorpions have a clever way to take in food. They discharge digestive juices from the gut into this cavity below their mouths, digest the food there and then consume it in liquid form. They trap the solid parts that can't be digested, like fur, in this cavity and spit it out.

- Many scorpion species are cannibals. If the male is not quick enough to go away after mating and lingers around to say adios, the female may attack him with her telson and kill him. She might even eat him after that. (The smarter male first grabs the claws of the female when he approaches her.) The *femme fatal* doesn't stop at eating her mate. She can eat her offspring too! Once the baby scorpions have hatched, they come out and climb up to her back. They remain there till the time they can feed themselves and grow a harder exoskeleton (they've quite soft ones at birth).

- When the baby scorpions are off her back, she may catch and eat one or two of the lot. The young scorpions usually avoid the elders and try not to cross their paths. But these babies are not that innocent either. In rare cases, even the little scorpions might eat their mother! Why does this happen? Scorpions developed this habit of eating other scorpions, including mates and children, to survive in severe conditions. What would you do if you were starving to death? Okay, you wouldn't eat your mum. Remember, scorpions are the first and longest surviving land animals. How do you suppose they achieved that?

WHAT ABOUT THE SCORPION HILL?

So now you know why naturalist Raza Tehsin was surprised when he went out on a walk in the jungle one day in 1979 and found thousands of scorpions living together on a small hillock. These scorpions had made slit-like holes big enough to house a single scorpion. The slits made neat lines all over the hill.

WHY ON EARTH?

Maybe the particular scorpion species had evolved in such a way that they learnt to live in harmony with each other. Or there was a fine leader among them who punished anyone who ate the other. Or Goddess Serket extracted a promise from them that they wouldn't eat their fellow scorpions.

But the most probable explanation for these aggressively predatory creatures staying together can be adaptation due to availability of food in a limited area or due to having a small habitat. There are always exceptions to the rule. A few scorpion species may even share burrows and food. The Emperor Scorpion, mainly a rainforest species from Africa, exhibits a degree of social behaviour like living in a colony.

So there are no 'rules' in nature. Predators can be prey and cannibals can live in colonies. Go figure!

STRIKING STING FACTS

* THE HONEY BEE WORKERS' STINGS ARE BARBED AND REMAIN STUCK IN THE FLESH OF THE VICTIM. THE WORKER BEE DIES WITHIN MINUTES AFTER STINGING! SO WHO'S THE VICTIM ACTUALLY?

* THE STINGRAY HAS A SERRATED BARB LOCATED IN ITS TAIL WHICH IT THRUSTS INSIDE THE ONE IT ATTACKS.

* THERE ARE VENOMOUS SPURS ON THE HIND LEGS OF THE DOCILE, MALE PLATYPUS.

* THE TARANTULA HAWK IS A WASP THAT HAS ONE OF THE MOST PAINFUL STINGS IN THE INSECT WORLD. WHAT ELSE CAN YOU EXPECT FROM SOMEONE WHO HUNTS TARANTULAS FOR FOOD?

* THE STING OF THE STONEFISH, ONE OF THE MOST VENOMOUS FISH IN THE WORLD, CAN BE LETHAL FOR HUMANS.

WHO HAS THE MOST UNUSUAL NEST OF ALL?

HOW WOULD YOU LIKE IT IF YOUR HOME WAS MADE OF BANANA
LEAVES, OR YOUR MUM'S AND DAD'S SALIVA, OR POOP?
DON'T WORRY, WE ARE NOT TALKING ABOUT DELIGHTFUL HUMAN
HOMES BUT STRANGE NESTS OF STRANGE CREATURES, INCLUDING
BIRDS. YES, APART FROM BIRDS, THERE ARE OTHER CREATURES
WHO BUILD NESTS. THEY DO SO NOT JUST WITH TWIGS AND LEAVES,
BUT BIZARRE, WEIRD THINGS CONSTRUCTED IN MYSTERIOUS WAYS.
LET'S TAKE A LOOK AT SOME OF THESE CREATURES AND
THEIR CRAZY NESTS.

HEARTY HORNBILLS

The hornbill is a bird which has a heavy horn-like bill—long, down-curved, sometimes brightly coloured with a casque on the top. A casque is an anatomical structure, just like a helmet.

The scientific name of this bird is derived from the Greek word *buceros* which means cow horn. There are fifty-five species of hornbills—some can be as small as a dove, others as large as a turkey!

The incredible bill is used for multiple purposes—feeding, building nests and even fighting snakes! The Great Pied Hornbill, with a wingspan of five feet, can swallow snakes like noodles. And mind you, they don't like humans spying on them or their nests under the pretext of research. If you're not using a blind to observe them, they might come and drop a branch on your head!

Different types of hornbills have different uses for the casque on their bills. In the Great Indian Hornbill's case, the casque is the horn on its bill. It has openings between the hollow centre and is used to make resonating calls.

In the Helmeted Hornbill, the casque is not hollow. It is filled with ivory and the bird uses it as a battering ram. That's cooler than a horn!

The Southern Ground Hornbill, which looks like a turkey, is the most carnivorous of all hornbills. Its beak is strong enough to open break the shell of a tortoise! Small groups of these hornbills move about in a line in the grass and in bushes, scanning the area for insects, scorpions and other such yummy delights.

Hornbills make a variety of sounds. The Great Indian Hornbill roars and barks. Helmeted Hornbills hoot and make a laughing sound. Von der Decken's Hornbills clucks. The booming call of the largest hornbill—Southern Ground—can be heard two to three miles away.

Their small tongues are not big enough to reach the end of their large beaks, where the food—fruits, figs and insects—is caught at times. So they toss it into their open mouths like popcorn.

Hornbills are birds of the Old World (remember the Old and the New World we spoke about?). They are pretty old themselves. They appeared fifteen million years ago. So naturally, there are many myths about them.

The hill tribes of Borneo believe that the Rhinoceros Hornbill delivers souls to the afterlife. There is a celebration in western Borneo every few years to honour hornbills. Rhinoceros Hornbills are associated with the god of war in Borneo.

Still, hornbills are hunted. Many species are endangered due to the humans invading their forest homes and destroying them.

NEST AT ITS BEST
Hornbills generally have only one mate for life and the nest they make is a mean feat. Let's see how they go about it.

Step 1: Find a crevice on a rock or a hole in a tree. If you can't find an empty one, fight the snake or monitor lizard occupying it and chase it out.

Step 2: The female should seal herself inside the hole. (All hornbill females, except the Southern Ground Hornbill and the Northern Ground Hornbill, seal themselves inside the nest. If you're one of the two, don't waste your time reading these instructions.) Now use droppings, soil, chewed wood, saliva and other such handy matter to make a wall (the male from outside and the female from inside). But don't forget to leave a slit open. The male will remain outside and pass the female food through this slit.

Step 3: Female hornbills should moult (like snakes and scorpions) once she is inside the hole. She should shed her feathers and regrow them only before she comes out again.

Step 4: While the female is trapped inside and is laying eggs, the male should supply food through the slit. The females of smaller species lay more eggs and incubate for a shorter period of time; the larger ones lay a couple of eggs and incubate them for a month and a half.

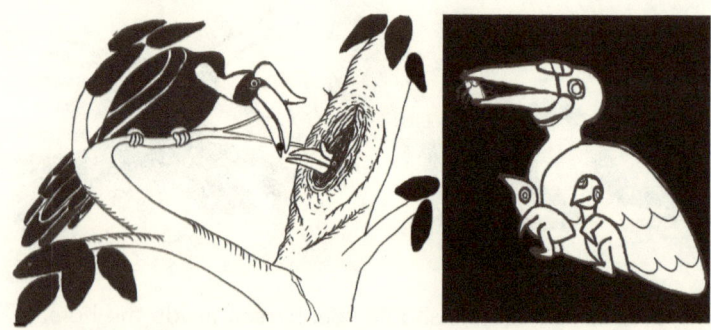

Step 5: Once the eggs have hatched, of some species females break the wall and come out, while others remain inside. If the female is out, both the male and the female feed the chicks together. Else the job is done by the male alone. Lizards, insects, berries are preferred food. Some larger hornbills can swallow fruits and then regurgitate them to the female, one at a time.

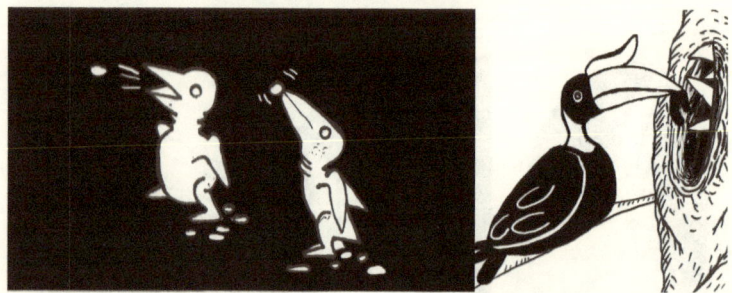

Step 6: Don't dirty the nest! The female should eject her excreta from the opening as far as possible. The chicks should be taught the same technique. Till the time the chicks aren't able to do so, the female should pick up their poop and throw it out.

Step 7: If something happens to the male, the whole family can die of hunger. So the female and chicks are advised not to be too cranky about what they want to eat and give the guy some breathing space!

MARVELLOUS MURREL

There is a fish that nests too!

It is the murrel or giant snakehead. The murrel is an elongated fish found in fresh water bodies like wetlands, lakes and rivers. It migrates to flooded fields and returns to its permanent home once the fields are dry. Humans prey on this fish and it is fished commercially wherever it is found. The murrel, in turn, preys on smaller fish, water bugs, frogs and suchlike.

Male and female murrels construct a nest out of water vegetation by biting the vegetation and making a doughnut-shaped nest, taking the additional help of their tails to shape it. The female lays eggs in it. Both the parents guard the eggs till they hatch. Dad is more vigilant of the two. Mum and Dad don't leave the reddish orange fry till they turn greenish brown. Did you think we're talking about frying the fish? No, no, no. We're talking of the little baby fish which are also called fry.

Fish undergo some pretty interesting growth stages.

STAGES OF FISH GROWTH

Stage 1: The egg

Stage 2: The larva: The yellow sac surrounding a larva provides them nutrition.

Stage 3: The fry: The sac disappears and the little fish are capable of feeding themselves.

Stage 4: The fingerling: The scales and fins are developed and the little ones are the size of fingers.

Stage 5: Fish

Murrels are pretty hot-headed and will attack anything moving around them when they're protecting their brood.

BROODING BROODS

The murrel brood moves like a dark cloud in the water. The female guides it and the male remains on the edge. He attacks and chases away other carnivorous fish, turtles, water snakes and even birds. The female might also attack the intruders. She guides the brood cautiously from one hiding place to another in shallow water, always keeping herself under the brood.

Murrels take oxygen from the air, so they have to come to the surface now and then to gulp a mouthful. When the little ones come to take air at the surface, parents remain on vigil. The male murrel with a brood has even been known to attack a low-flying pigeon, considering the poor bird a threat. The male murrel catapults out of the water and hits the pigeon. In the process it may end up on dry land, many feet away from the water and then has to struggle to get back into the lake.

So, as you can see, the parent murrels are very dedicated to their young and protect them till the time they're able to look after themselves. But even they eat one or two of their children now and then!

THE TERRIFIC TAILORBIRD

Cheeup-cheeup-cheeup...if you hear this song, it has to be the tailorbird singing! Though these small birds are generally hidden behind bushes, leaves and other vegetation, their loud call gives away their presence. They are insectivores. You may see them hopping on the grass in your garden, looking for grub.

You'll find them singing and hopping by forest edges, farmlands and urban gardens. The little bird is greenish in colour with an upright tail and a sharp bill which curves at the tip. This tip is not just a fancy addition to scare insects but it has a special purpose. And this is from where the tailorbird gets its name. It uses its pointed beak as a needle to sew its nest!

TAILORED NEST

The tailorbird is usually seen alone and roosts alone at night.

But if you see it hopping in a pair or roosting side by side that means it's their mating season.

Once the female lays the eggs (two to three) and incubates them for around twelve days, the eggs are ready to hatch. The hatchlings break the eggs, come out and remain in their tailor-made nest for around fourteen days. While both the parents are busy bringing the hungry hatchlings insects, a hungry lizard, cat, rat or crow pheasant may sneak up from behind and go away with a chick or two. Once the little ones fledge and are ready to take short flights, the parents teach them to fly and hunt. At night you may find the little fledglings sleeping, sandwiched between their mum and dad.

The tailorbird's nests are interesting to observe and you can easily locate them. But beware! Don't casually approach any nest made out of growing leaves in the garden. It can be the nest of stinging red weaver ants too! These ants, which are arboreal, live in colonies of thousands and build their nests by bending and weaving leaves together. From a distance, these can look just like the harmless nest of birds!

SWANKY SWIFTLETS

The swiftlet is a small bird with a slightly forked tail and boomerang-shaped wings. It belongs to the swift family, to which belong some of the world's fastest flying birds. The family's scientific name Apodiformes means without feet. (Which is the clever language from which the family name is derived? Yes... Greek.) Many of them have short legs and long wings and can't perch on a branch or ground with ease. Even if they manage to sit down, it is difficult for them to take off in flight. The easier thing to do is drop down from a cliff. So most of them prefer to eat, mate and even sleep in the air!

Scientists have studied the sleeping birds in flight and say that they flap their wings now and then to maintain height and speed. When they're awake, they do some amazing acrobatics in the air! Scientists study their flight in order to improve aircraft designs. Swifts hardly flap their wings when they glide or dive.

ECHOLOCATION

It is also called bio sonar. Animals that echolocate emit calls and wait for the echoes to come back to them. This way they can locate obstacles, even when it is pitch dark, and navigate with ease. They use echoes to locate prey and food as well. Echolocation is not found in too many birds. These birds are found in the tropics and sub-tropics. Most of them breed in dark caves and even roost there at night. Some swiftlets use simple echolocation, like bats, to navigate and locate their prey in total darkness. Unlike the echo of bats, which we can't hear, we can hear the clicking sound of swiftlets.

SUPER SALIVA

Swiftlets use their saliva to build nests! It takes more than a month to build a nest by a pair or a male alone. The bird produces a long strand of saliva, like a slippery, sticky noodle. It then bobs its head back and forth to dab the rock with its saliva and build the base of the nest. Then the noodle is wound into a cup-shaped nest on the vertical surface of a cave. The spit nest is white, spongy and sticky.

The little swiflets can't carry leaves or other such nesting materials to build their nest. But they do manage to bring in feathers, dried twigs or grass that they find floating in the air. Some species like the Edible-nest Swiftlet construct their nests entirely out of saliva. The nest looks like a mass of intricately knitted vermicelli.

Generally, the breeding takes place during the wet season, as there are a lot of insects to feed the young. Many species nest in colonies in high and dark caves. Both the mum and dad swiftlets take care of the young once they've come out of their eggs.

These dark caves, where bats may also cohabit with the swiftlets, have their own eco-systems. Some animals live on the guano or the droppings of bats and swiftlets. (Hmm…guano… fancy name for poop.) Other animals live on the bats and swiftlets themselves—like snakes and huge carnivorous crickets that feed on bat pups and swiftlet chicks.

But it's not just snakes that visit the swiftlets' nests. Who else does? Humans!

EDIBLE NESTS

Humans eat swiftlet nests! The Chinese have used it in their food for over 400 years. It is used in Chinese medicine as well. Bird's nest soup is a special delicacy made out of the solidified saliva of swiftlets. When the nest is dissolved in water, it becomes jelly-like in texture. A bowl of this swiftlet soup can cost anything between $30 to $100 in the United States. A kilo of top quality swiftlet nests can cost as much as half the price of gold!

Some other dishes in which bird's nest is used:

- Bird's nest jelly (ready-to-eat jelly also available in jars)
- Bird's nest boiled rice
- Deserts like egg tarts

Swiftlet nests are removed by humans once the birds and chicks leave the nest. (Some nasty ones might remove the nests with the chicks in it. That's not cool.) The nests of the Edible-nest Swiftlet or the White-nest Swiftlet are most in demand as they are made mostly of saliva and don't have other things like feathers mixed in it.

The nest is supposed to be very nutritious and is said to :

- Help in digestion
- Help those with asthma
- Improve focus
- Improve the immune system
- Improve one's voice (!)

FLYING TENANTS

In a small southern Thai town, building owners have decided to have flying tenants! They've left the buildings unoccupied for swiftlets to build their nests. Thousands of birds occupy the buildings. The clever owners earn much more money by harvesting the nests than by renting the buildings to humans.

THE KINKY KING COBRA

THE KING COBRA IS THE ONLY SNAKE IN THE WORLD THAT NESTS! YOU DO EXPECT SOME UNIQUE THINGS FROM THE WORLD'S LONGEST VENOMOUS SNAKE. IT CAN REACH A LENGTH OF 18.8 FEET AND CAN RAISE ONE-THIRD OF ITS BODY UPRIGHT WHEN CONFRONTED. JUST IMAGINE A GIANT STANDING IN FRONT OF YOU, READY TO ATTACK, ITS HOOD SPREAD OUT IN DEFENCE!

But cobras, including the kings, don't attack humans unless they are cornered. And then too, they might give you a 'dry-bite', that is, not choose to waste their venom on you. After all, you're not their food, are you? If someone is bitten, the antivenom that the person is treated with is also made from cobra venom!

King cobras live mainly on other snakes including ratsnakes, kraits and even other cobras. Their favourite home is the rainforest. But they also enter farmlands looking for ratsnakes. They don't belong to the genus *Naja* to which other cobras belong. Their genus name, *Ophiophagus,* is derived from…yes, you guessed it, ancient Greek, meaning snake eating. So the king cobra is a snake that eats snakes. Weird, huh?

Kings are good swimmers. But they can't escape the illegal wildlife trade and cutting down of forests by humans. With the thinning forests, king cobras are fading too. All they can do is hiss at this threat. Wait a minute, they don't hiss, they growl! Instead of a hiss, the king's deep-throated sound is often described as a growl.

COSY COBRA NEST

Oh yes, it *is* cosy. The nest is tightly constructed of leaves and twigs. Even during a heavy downpour it remains intact. The female lays twenty to forty eggs in the mound, which acts as an incubator. The eggs get warmth from the rotting vegetation while the female remains on top of the mound. The nest is unique and complex among snakes.

The female is a dedicated parent and guards the eggs ferociously for two to three months. But just when the eggs are about to hatch, the female abandons the nest. Remember, king cobras are snake eaters. She doesn't want to eat her own young, after all the time and energy she's spent on guarding them!

The little 45-cm-long cobras possess venom at birth that is as deadly as the adults'. It increases in quantity when they grow older. Although they're venomous and aggressive, many baby cobras don't see adulthood because they fall prey to mongooses, civets and even army ants!

As they grow, they lose their bright colours and become paler.

But wait...do you still want to know about *human* homes? There are a few interesting ones—made of ice and dung and mud and straw. Most others are made of weird manmade materials. We could talk about it sometime. But then the book wouldn't be called *Mysteries of Nature* now, would it?

AMAZING ANIMAL HOME FACTS

※ TERMITE MOUNDS IN THE TROPICAL SAVANNAHS CAN GROW UP TO 29.5 FEET IN HEIGHT! THEY HAVE THEIR OWN AIR-CONDITIONING AND CAN EVEN CONTAIN FUNGUS GARDENS INSIDE.

※ BEAVERS ARE EXPERT AND PROLIFIC BUILDERS AND BUILD DAMS OVER STREAMS.

※ THE LEAF-CURLING SPIDER CURLS A LEAF IN A FUNNEL LIKE FASHION AT THE CENTRE OF ITS WEB AND LIVES IN IT TO PROTECT ITSELF FROM PREDATORS.

※ SUBTERRANEAN ANT 'SUPERCOLONIES' HAVE BEEN REPORTED TO STRETCH OVER THOUSANDS OF KILOMETRES CONTAINING MILLIONS OF ANT NESTS.

※ GOPHERS, THE BURROWING RODENTS, CREATE A SOPHISTICATED NETWORK OF UNDERGROUND TUNNELS SPREAD OVER ACRES WHERE THEY COLLECT LARGE HOARDS OF FOOD.

IS THE OWL MAGICAL?

BLACK MAGIC, CURSES, GOOD AND BAD OMENS, THE ELUSIVE
PHILOSOPHER'S STONE... GUESS WHICH CREATURE IS COMMON TO
ALL THESE PRACTICES AND BELIEFS? THE OWL.
IT HAS BEEN ASSOCIATED WITH SORCERY AND
THE SUPERNATURAL FOR AGES. DOES THE OWL INDEED
HAVE MAGICAL POWERS? IF SO, WHAT ARE THEY? IF NOT,
WHY HAS IT BEEN CONNECTED WITH MAGIC FOR CENTURIES?

THE OWL IN INDIA

The owl is also associated with the Hindu goddess Laxmi. It is her steed. Athena, the Greek goddess of wisdom, is also accompanied by an owl. But as soon as you say *ulloo* (that's owl in Hindi) people shake their heads and smile. Why is owl a synonym for a fool in India when it is the symbol of wisdom in many other cultures?

In India, there is a lot of

ridicule for a bird which is very useful to humans and, well, pretty intelligent too. It seems that the answer lies in the competition between Laxmi (the goddess of wealth) and Saraswati (the goddess of knowledge). It is said that if Laxmi is happy with someone, Saraswati is annoyed with that person and vice versa. So if you have knowledge, you'll be poor and if you have wealth, you'll be a fool.

So the gifted yet poor writers vented their anger towards the rich favourites of Laxmi by calling her steed, the owl, names. They said that since the owl comes out at night and is a dimwit, it carries Laxmi to other fools like itself!

So those on Saraswati's team have called the owl a fool in their writings. But that's not all; the owl has been associated with dark magic and sorcery too, and used as a means to reach Laxmi (aka money!).

MANIC MAGIC AND FOUL OWL

WHERE IS THE PHILOSOPHER'S STONE?

LOONY

According to a widespread belief in India, the Indian Great Horned Owl has the philosopher's stone in its nest. This stone is supposed to turn base metals into gold just by touch. Some lazy people, who don't want to work hard, believe that all they've to do is recite mantras for five years, and on the eve of Diwali in the fifth year, locate the nest of the bird. They think by sacrificing an owl, they can obtain the philosopher's stone and turn all their metal doors and window grills, cooking pans and pots into gold! Of course, they're able to recite the mantras and kill the poor owl, but they can't find the stone. (Simply because there is no such stone!)

It is considered an ill omen if an owl sits near someone's home and imitates the sound of a crying baby. But it is a good omen if the owl sits there silently the whole night. Not just this, some folks even raise owls and then sacrifice them on so-called auspicious nights to use their flesh in magic, specially in curses.

Before we dig deeper to know the reason behind all this silly superstition, we need to understand what owls are.

OWESOME OWLS

- THEY ARE BIRDS OF PREY FOUND ALL OVER THE WORLD EXCEPT ANTARCTICA AND A FEW OTHER REMOTE PLACES. THERE ARE AROUND 200 DIFFERENT KINDS DIVIDED INTO TWO FAMILIES: BARN OWLS AND TYPICAL OWLS. ALL OWLS HAVE LARGE EYES ON THEIR FLAT FACES AND A FACIAL DISK (CIRCLE OF FEATHERS) AROUND EACH EYE. WHAT DIFFERENTIATES THE BARN OWL FROM THE TYPICAL OWL IS THEIR HEART-SHAPED FACE.

- THEY BUILD THEIR NESTS IN HOLLOWS OF TREES, OLD BUILDINGS OR BURROWS MADE IN THE GROUND.

- OWLS GENERALLY LIVE ALONE AND ARE ACTIVE AT NIGHT (NOCTURNAL). THEY HUNT INSECTS AND SMALL ANIMALS AND BIRDS. SOME ARE SPECIALIZED FISH HUNTERS. A BIG OWL CAN FINISH TWO TO THREE RATS A NIGHT.

- THEY HAVE FORWARD-FACING EYES (UNLIKE HAWKS AND OTHER BIRDS OF PREY WHO HAVE EYES ON THE SIDES OF THEIR HEAD) AND BINOCULAR VISION. IT HELPS THEM IN LOW-LIGHT HUNTING. SINCE THEIR EYES ARE FORWARD FACING, THEY NEED TO ROTATE THEIR HEADS TO CHANGE VIEWS.

- OWLS CAN ROTATE THEIR HEADS 270 DEGREES! THIS IS BECAUSE THEY HAVE FOURTEEN NECK VERTEBRAE AS COMPARED TO THE SEVEN IN HUMANS.

- OWLS ARE FARSIGHTED AND CAN'T SEE ANYTHING CLEARLY NEARBY. BUT THEY HAVE 'FEELERS' OR HAIR-LIKE FEATHERS ON THEIR BEAK AND

FEET TO FEEL THE PREY.

• THEY HAVE AN ALMOST NOISELESS FLIGHT. THE SILENT APPROACH DOESN'T GIVE ANY WARNING TO THE UNSUSPECTING LIZARD OR FROG. SURPRISE AND STEALTH ARE THE OWL'S HUNTING STRATEGIES. THEIR SMELLING AND HEARING SENSES ARE STRONG. IF NEED BE, ESPECIALLY IN PLACES WHERE THERE IS A SCARCITY OF PREY DUE TO SNOW, THEY HUNT IN THE DAYTIME.

OWL PELLETS

The owl's silent flight and dull colour help in hunting. But its sharp beak and powerful talons do the final job. The talons crush the skull and knead the body of the prey. Owls either swallow the prey whole or break it into pieces and gulp it down. They regurgitate their food. Whatever they can't digest, like fur, bones and scales, they throw out in the form of pellets. You can collect these pellets from under the trees and dissect them to know what the owl ate the night before.

THE INDIAN GREAT HORNED OWL

Is this owl really magical? It *does* have a spooky habit—it can talk in a human voice!

Like the hill myna, the Indian Great Horned Owl has the ability to mimic any sound or voice—human or otherwise. They're expert mimics and are the source of many a ghost story. Imagine you're walking alone in a jungle in the dead of the night and you hear a bloodcurdling scream or a woman chuckling—*heh…heh…heh*—but there is no one around. What will you come home and tell your mum (if you don't pass out in the jungle, that is)?

Most times, the mischief-maker is not a ghost or a witch but the Indian Great Horned Owl. Raza has had many such experiences in the forests where he came across these horned owls imitating noises and voices. These really do make good horror stories!

The other reason why sorcerers get impressed with this horned owl, (it is also called Eurasian Eagle-Owl), is its sheer size!

It is a very large and powerful bird, sometimes even referred as the world's largest owl. It has a bulky barrel-shaped body and ear tufts that stand upright and look like the horns of a devil. They can weigh more than 4 kg and their wingspan can reach up to 6.6 feet!

With such a large body, they not only hunt small animals like mice and rabbits but also bigger ones such as foxes and young deer. They also gorge on venomous snakes.

Here is something that Raza Tehsin once witnessed: One evening in 1988, Raza was standing under a mango tree in Chandesara village, near Udaipur. There were a lot of peacocks in this village. The sun had just set and many birds had already settled on the trees for the night. A full-grown peafowl with a long flowing tail flew down the hill and perched on top of the tree. An Indian Great Horned Owl suddenly came and struck the bird, which dropped to the ground with a thud. The owl took a long turn and came back to its prey. Before the owl could reach it, three pie-dogs dashed towards the peacock and tore it to pieces. The owl turned and flew away.

These owls are not very fussy about where they live and can inhabit the edge of a desert to forests and farmlands. They generally choose caves, cliff ledges and crevices to nest.

There is hardly any animal which can hunt an Indian Great Horned Owl except man, who kills it for crazy things like black magic and finding the philosopher's stone.

MORE MAD MYTHS

Owls have not only been associated with foolishness and wisdom, but with some crazy things as well:

In the Middle East, owls are considered a bad omen. In Kenya, Africa, they are considered a harbinger of bad luck, ill health and death.

In the Americas, the Mayans thought owls brought death and destruction. The Hopis associated them with sorcery and the Mexicans believed that when the owl cries a (Native) Indian dies.

So these are the mad myths that do the rounds around the world. But the owl is actually an awfully useful bird. How?

Not long ago, the wealth of humans was measured by the amount of food and clothes they had. Mice are the biggest destroyers of this wealth. Laxmi's steed, the owl, eats mice and keeps their population under control. So let's stop calling it foolish and evil and what-not. It is a fine bird that we hope will live long and prosper!

OWLS IN LITERATURE

* HEDWIG IS HARRY POTTER'S PET OWL.
* IN WINNIE-THE-POOH STORIES, THE OWL IS QUITE KNOWLEDGEABLE, YET SPELLS INCORRECTLY.
* IN *POGO*, HOWLAND OWL IS THE SELF-PROCLAIMED EXPERT IN ALL FIELDS.
* WISE OWL IS THE WISE ONE IN *LITTLE GREY RABBIT*, BUT CAN BE QUITE FINICKY IN THE DAYTIME WHEN DISTURBED.
* MASTER GLIMFEATHER CALLS HIS 'PARLIAMENT' OF OWLS IN THE SILVER CHAIR TO DISCUSS MATTERS OF IMPORTANCE IN *THE CHRONICLES OF NARNIA*.

WHY DOES THE KOEL SING?

DO YOU KNOW WHERE THE WORD KOEL IS DERIVED FROM? NO, THIS TIME YOU'RE WRONG. IT'S NOT ANCIENT GREEK. IT IS SANSKRIT! THE NAME IS DERIVED FROM THE SANSKRIT WORD *KOKILA*. IT IS ALSO CALLED KOKILA IN MARATHI AND BENGALI. IT IS POPULARLY BELIEVED ACROSS CULTURES AND COUNTRIES THAT THE SWEET KOOOO-OOO SOUND IT MAKES COMES FROM THE FEMALE BIRD. IS THIS TRUE?

THE KOEL'S SONG

From ancient times, the koel has found an important place in Indian literature, in poetry and in myths. It also has a very special place in tribal lore and traditions. Not just in India, in Sri Lanka, the koha's (Sinhalese name for koel) song is supposed to be the herald of the traditional new year. It is held in high regard in

scriptures like the Manusmriti, which has an ancient decree to protect them.

The word 'koel' brings with it the feel of a summer dusk in a forest and a soft trembling note floating upon the sweet scent of mango flowers. Or an intoxicating chirp carried in the breeze in the pale dawn.

CLASSY KOELS

What is the koel? It is a kind of cuckoo. The Asian Koel is a large long-tailed cuckoo found in South and Southeast Asia and China. It lives almost all over India and has great adaptability to new areas.

Let's check how much we know about this bird.

TRUE OR FALSE?

1. A koel looks like a crow.
2. Koels love boiled eggs.
3. Koels have a noiseless flight.
4. Koels have a sequence of sixteen notes.
5. The singing koel is a female.

Ans. 1 False...almost.

The male koel is black in colour but is different in build from a crow. In size it is a little smaller and thinner than a crow, but with a longer tail. Unlike crows, where male and females look alike, koels have sexual dimorphism, that is, males and females look very different. The male koel is glossy black with red eyes and the female is dark brown with white spots and streaks. Koels, like royalty or celebrity, don't like to be spotted and live in thick trees, groves and woods. They are solitary birds.

Ans. 2 Not really.

For food, this bird mostly has small fruits, various kinds of berries and even millipedes and eggs (not boiled ones!) of smaller birds. Since the adults feed mainly on fruits, they are important for the seed dispersal of many plants and trees, especially sandalwood. These birds were once quite popular as cage-birds and even survived on boiled rice! They lived up to fourteen years in captivity.

Ans. 3 True.

Like the owl, the koel has quite a noiseless flight. Since it is a very silent bird, its presence is known only when it flies small distances from one tree to the other looking for fruits. It passes the cold winter days in silence but as soon as summer starts, this bird becomes chirpy and cheery. This is also its mating season. In the cooler mornings and evenings of summer, and even during the rains, the rising note of the koel's kooo-oooo can be heard everywhere.

Ans. 4 False.

The koel's melodic and unique sequence has seven to eight notes. It starts its chirp by a shrill note and repeats it in twos. Every note rises to a higher pitch. When it reaches its seventh or eighth chirp, the note is at its highest peak and then it breaks. But the koel starts the note again quickly in the same harmony and rhythm. People are captivated by the rising and falling notes of a koel's call.

Ans. 5 FALSE (in capital letters!)

Can you imagine that in spite of such flowery language, high regard, praises and admiration, a grave injustice has been done to this bird? The sweet voice, which everyone is familiar with, is the voice of the *male* koel! And we have always believed it to be female! There's even a word, *kokilakanthi,* meaning a female singer with the voice of a koel. Turns out, it's the male koel who sings!

Koels have other chirping notes too. The male goes to his territory at the break of dawn and starts chirping. It is a flat shrill note—udak-ke-oo, ke-oo, ke-oo—which is repeated seven times. This is to make the other male koels aware of his presence and his territory. When he finds a mate and follows her, she jumps from branch to branch in a mock chase and chirps kik-kik-kik in

her shrill voice (yes, that shrill voice is the voice of female koel!).
At times, this twittering is intercepted by a sharp piercing ka-da-
da-da peep, resembling the peep of a crow's chicks. The koel
sings the whole day to attract a mate. Its melodious notes are
heard only in its mating season, mainly between April to August.
It is silent in the winter but becomes more and more vocal as
summer approaches. It can be one of the earliest bird voices you
hear on a summer dawn.

BROOD PARASITES

The mention of crows brings us to a nasty trait of the koel. It is
a brood parasite! The Vedas, written thousands of years ago, refer
to koels as *anya-vapa* meaning 'one raised by others'. By others we
mean mostly crows and sometimes birds like mynas. This musical
bird, so highly respected, has a mean habit. It never builds its own
nest and sneaks into the nest of the crow or some other bird to
lay its eggs. Sometimes, during the koel's mating season, which
is almost at the same time as the crow's, you might come across a
female koel and a female crow pushing and shoving each other in
a fight. This is when the female koel tries to sneak into the crow's
nest to lay its eggs. If it's spotted by the female crow, it tries to
push the intruder away.

Koel and crow eggs are quite similar, though the koel's are a
bit smaller in size. Sometimes, the male distracts the female crow
while its mate sneaks in and lays the eggs. But most of the times,
the female approaches the nest alone. The koel lays one or two
eggs in the nest at a time. There are two reasons why a koel finds
it convenient to lay her eggs in a crow's nest:

1. A crow's nest is big enough to hold twelve to thirteen
    eggs at a time.
2. The koel chick are initially similar in colour to those of the
    crow's.

The poor female crow ends up incubating the koel's eggs
and feeding the koel's chicks. Koel's eggs take lesser time to

hatch than crow's eggs. While it takes thirteen to fourteen days for a koel's eggs to hatch, a crow's takes sixteen to seventeen days. The jungle crow's eggs take even longer to hatch. So the chicks of the koel, who initially call like crows, get a three-day advantage— it eats all the food brought in by the confused crow mum, who thinks they're her chicks.

That's not all. Koels can lay eggs in the nests of much smaller birds too. Once the eggs are hatched, the little birds are taken aback. The hatchlings are larger than the mum and dad birds! Not able to understand what has gone wrong, they continue to feed the hatchlings. Sometimes, when the tiny bird is feeding the hatchling larger than itself, it seems as if the hatchling could swallow its foster mother! The female koel keeps a watch and sometimes sneaks in to feed its chicks. They fledge after twenty to twenty-eight days.

The cleverness of the fox is legendary. And so is the crow's. Here again the koel has not got its due. No one speaks of the cunning of the koel, who's able to fool the clever crow into parenting its chicks!

BROODING BROOD PARASITE FACTS

❋ CUCKOO BEES ARE BROOD PARASITES WHICH LAY THEIR EGGS IN THE NESTS OF OTHER BEES. THERE IS A BROOD PARASITE CUCKOO WASP TOO!

❋ CHICKS OF COWBIRDS, A BROOD PARASITE, CAN KILL THEIR NESTMATES IF THE SUPPLY OF FOOD IS NOT SUFFICIENT FOR THEM. BUT IF THE FOOD BROUGHT IN BY THE FOSTER PARENTS IS ENOUGH, THEY DON'T RESORT TO KILLING.

❋ SOME BIRDS ARE SMART AND DON'T FALL FOR OTHER BIRDS LAYING EGGS IN THEIR NEST. AMERICAN COOTS CAN KICK THE PARASITE EGGS OUT OF THEIR NEST OR GO AND BUILD ANOTHER NEST OF THEIR OWN. THEY EVEN PECK THE PARASITE CHICKS OR DROWN THEM! IT IS NOTABLE THAT THE AMERICAN COOTS THEMSELVES ARE KNOWN TO LAY EGGS IN THE NEST OF OTHERS SOMETIMES!

❋ SOME BIRDS NEST TOGETHER AS A GROUP STRATEGY OF DEFENCE AGAINST BROOD PARASITISM. THE BROWN-HEADED COWBIRD IS NOT REALLY CHOOSEY AND CAN BE THE BROOD PARASITE TO UP TO 221 DIFFERENT HOSTS!

HOW IS A PIT VIPER SIMILAR TO A HEAT-SEEKING MISSILE?

A PIT VIPER IS NOT A VIPER *IN* A PIT BUT A VIPER *WITH* A PIT. AND A HEAT-SEEKING MISSILE IS, WELL, A HEAT-SEEKING MISSILE. ALSO KNOWN AS HEAT-SEEKERS, THESE MISSILES FOLLOW TARGETS WHICH EMIT INFRARED RADIATIONS. INFRARED IS RADIATED STRONGLY BY HOT BODIES LIKE JET ENGINES. THERE IS A DEEP CONNECTION BETWEEN THIS MISSILE AND THE SNAKE (YES, THE PIT VIPER IS A SNAKE). WHAT IS THE LINK BETWEEN THE DEADLY SNAKE AND THE DEADLY MISSILE? NO, IT'S NOT 'DEADLY.' IT IS SOMETHING QUITE FASCINATING.

SNAKES AND LIZARDS

Snakes are such remarkable and terrifying creatures—long, legless, carnivore reptiles. They are different from legless lizards though.

A SIMPLE FIELD GUIDE

TO SEE THE DIFFERENCE BETWEEN THE TWO, PICK UP A SNAKE IN ONE HAND AND A LEGLESS LIZARD IN ANOTHER.

THE LIZARD HAS EXTERNAL EARS AND WILL BLINK THEIR EYELIDS AT YOU. THE SNAKE HAS NEITHER AND WILL KEEP STARING.

SEE, SIMPLE!

(TIP: THE SNAKE MAY BITE/ATTACK YOU TO FREE ITSELF AND MIGHT NOT JUST KEEP STARING AT YOU. IN THAT CASE, JUST DROP THE IDEA AND DROP THE SNAKE TOO!)

If the snake wants to catch some sleep, it either closes its retina or buries its head in the folds of its body. It has clear scales that cover the eyes.

Also, most snakes have more joints in their skull than lizards. This helps them to swallow prey much larger than their heads. After all, snakes don't chew like us, they swallow.

Snakes are strictly carnivorous. Some snakes like vipers and cobras use venom to kill the prey. What's venom? It is modified saliva injected through fangs. It is *not* poison and they are not poisonous snakes. What's the difference? The difference is that poison is inhaled or ingested (smelled or eaten) and venom is injected. So there are venomous and non-venomous snakes, not poisonous and non-poisonous snakes.

THE LONGEST VENOMOUS SNAKE IS THE KING COBRA.
THE ONE WITH THE LONGEST FANGS IS THE BOMBA.
THE MOST VENOMOUS IS THE BLACK MAMBA.
THE LARGEST SNAKE IS THE RETICULATED PYTHON.
THE HEAVIEST IS THE ANACONDA.

The pit viper doesn't have any such distinction among snakes, but it has a pit...sorry, a bit of something special.

THE PITTED PIT VIPER

To understand what's special about pit vipers, we'll need to understand the senses use snakes:

EYESIGHT

The sharpness of eyesight may vary in different kinds of snakes. But it is generally not that sharp. It lifts its body and stands upright at times to get a wider view and survey the area.

VIBRATIONS

Since it doesn't have external ears (how much do you expect the fellow to hear with ears that are hidden somewhere inside?) and good vision, the snake depends on vibrations to sense

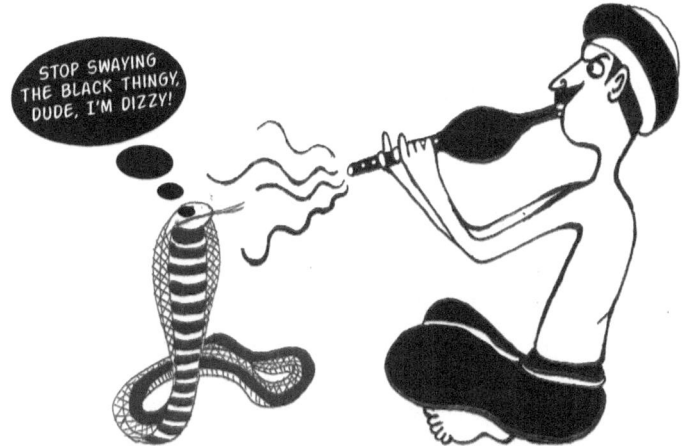

movement of other animals. If a large of part of your body were in direct contact with the ground, perhaps you, too, would be sensitive to vibrations.

Snakes are hard of hearing. So if you see a snake swaying to the music of a snake charmer, it is not because it can hear it, but because of the movement of the musical instrument which the charmer keeps swaying.

SMELL

Snakes smell through their forked tongues! The tongue collects airborne particles and sends it to the Jacobson's organ in the snake's mouth for examination. The tongue of water snakes like the anaconda functions well under water.

INFRARED

A few snakes like pit vipers, pythons and boas can 'see' the heat of warm-blooded animals. They do this with the help of the deep grooves that they have in their snout.

And this is what makes the pit vipers special. They have a sixth sense.

SLY SIXTH SENSE

There are around 151 kinds of vipers that form the group of pit vipers. Pit vipers are found in a variety of habitats—from deserts to thick jungles. All of them have a pit in common—a heat (or infrared) sensitive organ located between the eyes and the nostrils on each side of the head. These pits are actually openings to very sensitive infrared detecting organs. Pit vipers generally hunt at night. So this sense gives them a special advantage to 'see' in the dark. This sixth sense helps them form an image of the prey through its body heat. The snake tracks the prey and attacks it using this sense. The fangs in its upper jaw are movable and move forward before the snake bites (and fold back when not in use). It generally injects some venom into the prey and waits for it to die Once it is dead, it swallows the prey at leisure.

Did you know that all rattlesnakes are pit vipers? The eyelash viper is also a pit viper. Most kinds of rattlesnakes get together in dens or shelters to take advantage of the combined heat in winters. Sometimes you'll find up to 1,000 rattlesnakes hibernating together!

Scientists developed heat-seeking missiles using the same method that the pit vipers use. Defence researchers continue to study the pit viper's search-and-destroy mechanism to further develop missile detectors.

Snakes are not only useful for those developing missiles (if you consider missile development useful, that is) but in many other ways too.

To understand that, we need to get over, or at least keep aside, our fear of snakes. (An abnormal fear of snakes is called ophidiophobia.)

MAD MYTHS

Most of us fear snakes, although not all of us have ophidiophobia. These legless, eyelid-less, venomous or venom-less reptiles have always stirred fear in humans. There is probably no other creature which we have associated more with myths, stories, the supernatural and evil.

In ancient Egypt, an image of the Nile Cobra was to be found on the crown of the Pharaoh. It was also used in ritual suicide or to kill an enemy. Cleopatra used a snake to kill herself. Or was she killed using a snake? Historians are still unsure.

In ancient Greece, a serpent was considered a healer and worshipped.

In the Bible, the serpent lures Adam and Eve with the forbidden fruit.

In India, Lord Shiva has a snake wound around his neck. In fact, the snake appears in many Hindu myths and legends. Lord Krishna is said to have danced atop the multi-headed serpent Kalia. And when the gods and asuras set about churning the ocean in order to get the elixir of life, amrita, they used a serpent, Sheshnaga, to churn the ocean with. In fact, snakes are worshipped in parts of India and offered milk on Nag Panchami. This is a false belief though, as milk is not a part of the snake's diet. It is *strictly* non-vegetarian!

Have you heard the story of the avenging king cobra? The one you can't mess with? If you kill a cobra, your picture remains in its eyes. Later, its mate sees the picture of the murderer (you!) in the eyes of its dead partner and comes back for revenge. That is why snakes are burnt after they are killed, so no evidence of the murder can be found!

There is a basis to this wild story. During the breeding season, snakes release pheromones, a certain kind of chemical, to attract a mate. The pheromones can be smelt by other snakes for quite some distance. When a snake is killed, it gets agitated and releases a much larger quantity of pheromones. So even if a snake is dead, the smell of pheromones draws another snake to it. Of course, once it realizes that the dead snake is not responding, it just leaves and doesn't come back. But of course we all like to believe the more ghastly stories, don't we?

SPLENDID SNAKES

Of the 200+ kinds of snakes found in India, only five are deadly venomous. But we fear and kill them all. And we worship them on Nag Panchami. What's with the whole confusion?

In the past, a person was considered wealthy if she or he had a lot of food grains and cloth. Mice loved to gorge on both of these. And snakes gorged on mice. You might recall snakes protecting hidden treasures in many stories. Households kept a place for snakes so that they would protect their treasures of food grains and cloth from mice. And if you're wondering what a puny mouse can do, let's take a look, shall we?

ROWDY RODENTS

For every one man, there are six mice in India. Six mice eat one man's food. Their incisors, the two long teeth in the front, grow lifelong. To chisel them in position, they have to nibble constantly. So they waste more than they eat. Many people die each year due to diseases caused by mice. How many die of hunger caused by mice eating millions of tons of food grains is not even counted.

Owls, eagles etc. are predators of mice. Mice hide in their burrows to avoid them. But they can't avoid a snake in their burrow! This is important because otherwise, mice would reproduce too quickly. A pair of mice bred in ideal conditions can produce up to 880 mice a year. If this continues for five years, we can stack them one above the other and the height of this stack will be from the earth to the moon!

So how did the conflict between snakes and humans start and how do mice enter the picture? As the human population grew and people began cutting down forests, snakes were driven out of their usual habitats and began to enter human homes for shelter. In British India, there was an all-out campaign to kill snakes. However, better sense prevailed when they found that the mice population drastically increased as a result of this. The campaign was called off but by then, thousands of snakes had died. In Ratnagiri, Maharashtra alone, 28,000 snakes were killed.

Even after this, snakes keep getting killed illegally for their skin. With the snake population on the decline, the government decided to exterminate mice by poisoning them. However, the poisoned mice were eaten by eagles and owls, and they began to die of the poison too! That again meant fewer natural predators of mice and the mice population rose.

So there are better things to do with snakes than to study them to develop heat-seeking missiles for wars. For one, native non-poisonous snakes can be released in farms and food grain storages to tackle the destruction of food grains by mice.

This will help conserve snakes too.

STARTLING SNAKE FACTS:

* THE ROUGH-SCALED BUSH VIPER OF CENTRAL AFRICA IS A VENOMOUS SNAKE THAT HAS BRISTLE-LIKE SCALES, GIVING IT A FEATHERY APPEARANCE!

* THE HORNED VIPER IS A SANDY DESERT VIPER FROM NORTH AFRICA WITH ONE HORN OVER EACH EYE! THE HORNS ARE SCALES WHICH CAN FOLD BACK ON STIMULUS.

* THERE IS A FLYING SNAKE TOO! FOUND IN SOUTHEAST ASIA, A FLYING SNAKE DOESN'T ACTUALLY FLY BUT GLIDES IN THE AIR.

✳ THE TENTACLED SNAKE, FOUND IN SOUTHEAST ASIA, IS A MARINE SNAKE. IT IS THE ONLY SNAKE WITH TWO TENTACLES ON ITS SNOUT!

✳ THE ELEPHANT TRUNK SNAKE IS AN AQUATIC SNAKE WHICH HAS QUITE AN UNUSUAL SKIN THAT HANGS IN BAGS AND FOLDS, LOOKING TOO BIG FOR THE REPTILE!

DO TIGERS AND LEOPARDS DRINK BLOOD?

MUCH INK HAS BEEN SPENT ON THE SUBJECT OF WHETHER A TIGER OR LEOPARD SUCKS THE BLOOD OF ITS PREY. MOST NATURALISTS OF THE NINETEENTH CENTURY AND FIRST HALF OF THE TWENTIETH CENTURY WERE OF THE OPINION THAT THEY DO.

IS THAT TRUE? DO THESE BIG CATS FIRST DRINK THE BLOOD OF THEIR VICTIMS TO QUENCH THEIR THIRST BEFORE THEY GO AHEAD AND DEVOUR THEM?

FIRST LET'S GET A WEE BIT ACQUAINTED WITH THE TIGER AND THE LEOPARD TO KNOW IF IT'S A TRUTH OR A LIE.

TERRIFYING TIGERS

The tiger is a richly coloured striped big cat. It can be found as high as 10,000 feet in the Himalayas as well as in steamy evergreen forests, in the grassy swamps of Terai and the muddy and watery Sunderbans, where it leads an almost amphibious life.

Tiger needs three things to live comfortably:

- Lot of shade to sleep
- Lot of water to drink and chill in
- Lot of large animals to prey upon

Tigers hunt between sunset and dawn and sometimes on cloudy days as well, when it's not that bright. It can kill large

animals like female or young elephants, gaurs and wild buffaloes. If there is nothing to eat, it kills and eats smaller animals, and even dead ones!

Tigers love water! In spite of their heavy build, they are amazing swimmers. They also likes to sit and laze around in water pools in summer.

The movement of tigers and leopards depends on the season and availability of prey. In the monsoons, water is available everywhere and the prey scatters. The cats also wander in search of prey. In the summers, water is restricted to a few waterholes and streams, where the prey concentrates. So the movement of the cats is also restricted.

In a lifespan of approximately twenty years, around two are spent with their mum. Both leopard and tiger cubs are born blind and helpless. The mum carries them with her teeth, holding the loose skin on their neck whenever they wander away from the lair. Domestic cats do the same. Once they're six months old, the cubs accompany the tigress on hunting trips. If the tigress is a cattle-lifter or a man-eater, the cubs may learn the same things. That may explain the occurrences (in days when there were enough tigers) of man-eaters in the same regions again and again.

Tigers, like leopards, hide their kill if they can't finish eating the larger animals at once. Sometimes they hide it in boulders, sometimes in bushes or under leaves and grass if there is no other place to hide it. A panther may even lift the kill and hide it in a tree. There are too many other creatures around on the lookout for an easy meal. These hangers-on try to find and finish a tiger's or leopard's kill when they're not around.

The earliest known fossils of the tiger are from the New Siberian Islands. Tigers migrated from the north and reached the Himalayas first and colonized the mountains. But it seems they were too late in reaching the southern tip of India. The fact that they couldn't reach Sri Lanka suggests that the land bridge that once connected the island to India was no longer there. King cobras and flying lizards are amongst the other animals who couldn't cross over to Sri Lanka.

TIGER AND MAN

There are many folklores and legends about tigers. Humans have worshipped them. When a man is killed by a tiger, a red-painted stone, like a small deity, is placed at the spot. People worship it so that they don't meet the same fate.

According to another common belief, the spirit of the killed person rides the tiger that has killed him or her. The spirit warns the tiger of approaching danger.

Tigers are illegally killed not only for their skin, but also for some nutty beliefs:

TIGER FAT: CURES RHEUMATISM

TIGER BONE: USED AS CHARMS

TIGER CLAWS: ORNAMENTS

TIGER WHISKERS: LOVE CHARMS

TIGER LIVER: EATEN FOR COURAGE

MILK OF A TIGRESS: SOOTHES EYE PROBLEMS

LANKY LEOPARDS

Leopards are lanky, yes. And that's why many people confuse them with cheetahs. But these are two different cats. The cheetah is sleeker in built, and has black solid spots as opposed to the black rosettes of the leopard and runs and chases the prey, unlike a leopard, who stalks and attacks.

THE LEOPARD IS A SLEEK, SHORT-HAIRED CAT. ITS FUR IS SHORTER AND PALER IN THE DESERT AND LONGER IN THE SNOW LEOPARD FOUND IN KASHMIR. THIS CAT IS FOUND ALL OVER THE COUNTRY AND CAN LIVE IN ANY CLIMATE—DRY, HUMID, HOT OR COLD. IT DOESN'T HAVE THE MANY REQUIREMENTS THAT TIGERS HAVE TO LIVE COMFORTABLY. IT CAN LIVE IN OPEN COUNTRY AND AMONG ROCKS AND SHRUBS TOO.

LEOPARDS CAN HUNT BY DAY (IF THEY CAN'T AT NIGHT) AND SURVIVE ON DEER, BIRDS, REPTILES, CRABS AND EVEN MICE. IF THEY LIVE NEAR HUMAN SETTLEMENTS, THEY ALSO FEED ON CATTLE AND DOGS. THEY BREED ALL YEAR ROUND.

It's clear that leopards are quite adaptable and most successful in extending and maintaining their territory. According to fossil evidence, they too came from the north like the tigers. Maybe they arrived before the tigers because they could cross over to Sri Lanka via the land bridge.

The leopard's chief enemy is the tiger. The tiger can chase it away from its kill and even kill the leopard. But the leopard doesn't take it lying down. They are known to hunt tiger cubs if the tigress is not in sight.

The leopard also has immense strength. It can carry a full grown stag up a tree, just holding it in its jaws!

And leopards are very smart too. In fact, familiarity with man and his ways makes leopards a much more dreaded man-eater than tigers!

FALSE FABLE

TIGERS AND LEOPARDS DO NOT DRINK BLOOD. IT WAS BELIEVED FOR A LONG WHILE THAT THEY DO. BUT NOW, IT IS A KNOWN FACT THAT THESE CARNIVORES DO NOT HAVE ANY MECHANISM TO SUCK BLOOD WHEN THEY KILL THEIR PREY. THE SOLID, TAPERED (CONICAL) CANINES ARE SO TIGHTLY FIXED ON THE THROAT OR NAPE OF THE PREY THAT THERE IS NO SPACE FOR BLOOD TO BE SPILLED OUT OR TO BE SUCKED.

Naturalists have written a lot to establish that these cats don't suck blood. But why did this false notion come into being? Raza spent some time thinking about it and observed the hundreds of leopards that he has come across in the wild. He finally came up with this list:

1. These cats, by instinct, keep a tight hold on the prey for a long time even after the struggle stops, perhaps to make sure that it is dead. Since death is caused by choking, the prey becomes unconscious and might struggle again if the grip is released early. So that's why a tiger or leopard hangs on for a long while even after the struggle is over. This may have made some naturalists and hunters believe

that the big cat is sucking blood.

2. If you hold something tight in your mouth for long, there will be a lot of saliva. When the prey is gripped for a long time under the force of the upper and the lower jaws, the leopard's and tiger's mouths start to dribble. When the cat gulps this saliva it gives the false impression that it is sucking blood.

3. These cats spend a lot of their energy in stalking prey and lose a good amount of body fluid by perspiration. Once it kills the prey, the cat gets the mental satisfaction of having secured its food and its thirst overpowers its hunger. Many times it leaves the kill at a secure place and goes to drink water or rest. This habit made some naturalists (falsely) conclude that after sucking blood the beast has satisfied its hunger for the time being.

4. Lastly, a tiger or a panther doesn't normally eat its kill immediately after hunting. Perhaps it lets it rot a bit since decomposed meat is softer to tear. This delay is not because the beast has satisfied its hunger by sucking blood.

So tigers and leopards don't suck blood. They never have!

TERRIFIC TIGER FACTS

* THE TIGER IS THE LARGEST LIVING CAT SPECIES ON EARTH.

* A LIGER IS A CROSS BETWEEN A LION AND A TIGER! AND IT IS HUGE! LIGERS ENJOY SWIMMING LIKE TIGERS.

* THE COLOUR OF THE TIGER'S EYES IS YELLOW. BUT WHITE TIGERS GENERALLY HAVE BLUE EYES. THERE IS EVEN A GEMSTONE CALLED TIGER'S EYE!

* A LARGE CROC MAY TRY TO PREY UPON A TIGER. IF SEIZED BY A CROCODILE, A TIGER

STRIKES IT ON ITS EYES WITH ITS PAWS.

❋ LIKE FINGERPRINTS ARE USED TO IDENTIFY HUMANS, THE STRIPES OF A TIGER ARE ALSO UNIQUE TO EACH OF THEM AND ARE USED TO IDENTIFY IT.

LOVELY LEOPARD FACTS

❋ THE SNOW LEOPARD IS ALSO KNOWN AS THE 'GREY GHOST' AS IT IS VERY SECRETIVE AND STAYS WELL CAMOUFLAGED. IT MIGHT STAND STARING YOU IN THE FACE AT A DISTANCE, BUT YOU MIGHT NOT SEE IT!

❋ THE CLOUDED LEOPARD IS NOT A LEOPARD BUT A MYSTERIOUS CAT SOMEWHERE BETWEEN THE BIG CATS THAT ROAR AND THE SMALL CATS THAT PURR. IT MIGHT BE THE EVOLUTIONARY LINK BETWEEN THE TWO.

❋ A MAN-EATING LEOPARD CAN BE MUCH DEADLIER THAN A MAN-EATING TIGER! BECAUSE OF ITS STEALTH AND ITS CONTACT WITH HUMAN HABITATS, IT CAN BE AMAZINGLY CUNNING. THE MAN-EATING LEOPARD OF RUDRAPRAYAG WAS THE MOST DIFFICULT MAN-EATER IN JIM CORBETT'S HUNTING LIFE!

❋ THE LEOPARD'S TAIL CAN BE AS LONG AS ITS BODY!

❋ THERE IS A 'STRAWBERRY' LEOPARD IN A GAME RESERVE IN SOUTH AFRICA, WHICH HAS AN UNUSUAL REDDISH COLOUR! IT IS DUE TO A LESSER KNOWN AND UNUSUAL KIND OF PIGMENTATION IN THE LEOPARD'S SKIN.

ACKNOWLEDGEMENTS

Thank you, Fatema Tehsin, for being the home we could return to after each adventure and misadventure.

.